Tornado Slim
and the Magic Cowboy Hat

written and illustrated by
Bryan Langdo

Marshall Cavendish Children

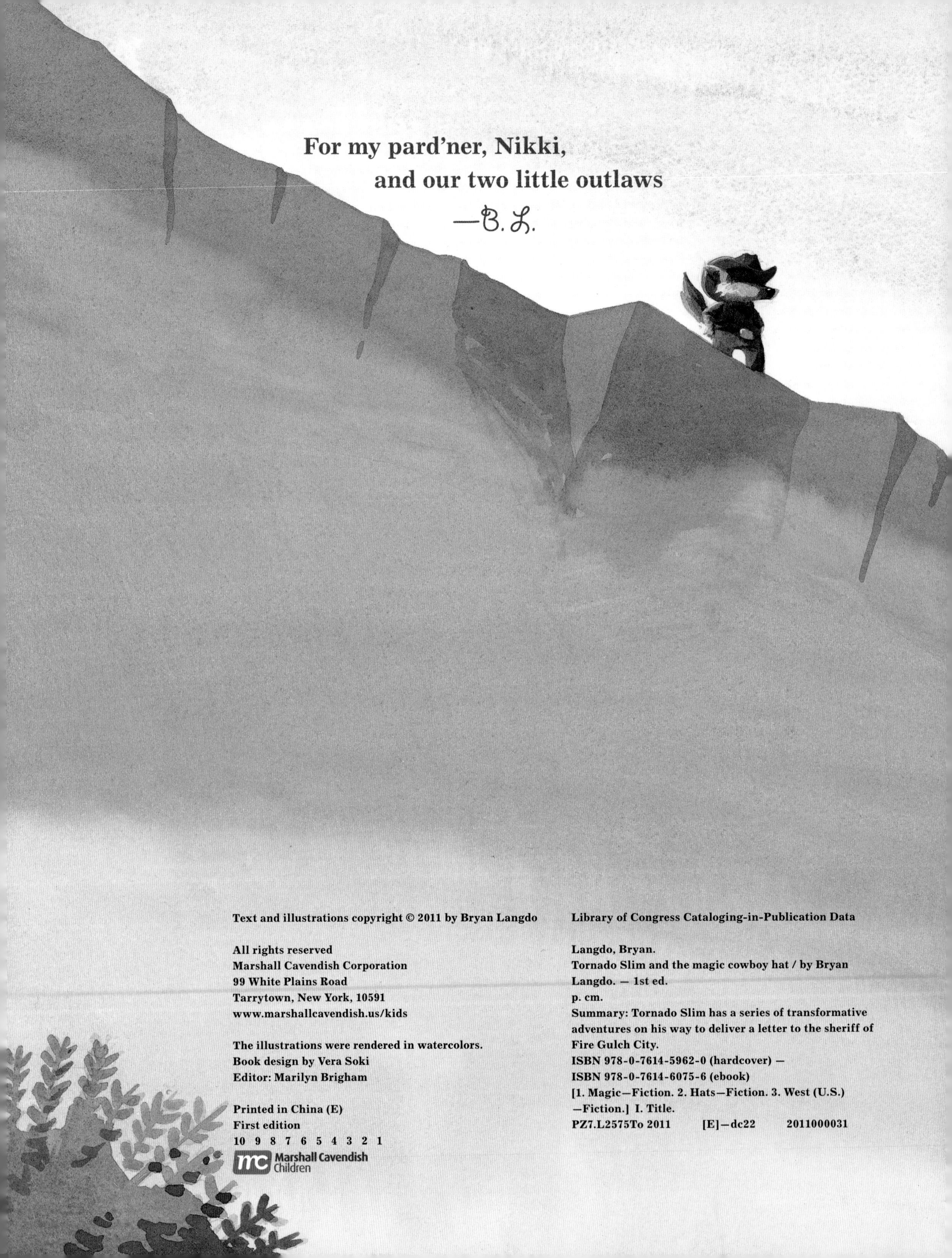

For my pard'ner, Nikki,
and our two little outlaws
—B. L.

Marshall Cavendish Corporation
99 White Plains Road
Tarrytown, New York, 10591
www.marshallcavendish.us/kids

The illustrations were rendered in watercolors.
Book design by Vera Soki
Editor: Marilyn Brigham

Printed in China (E)
First edition
10 9 8 7 6 5 4 3 2 1
Marshall Cavendish Children

Library of Congress Cataloging-in-Publication Data

Langdo, Bryan.
Tornado Slim and the magic cowboy hat / by Bryan Langdo. — 1st ed.
p. cm.
Summary: Tornado Slim has a series of transformative adventures on his way to deliver a letter to the sheriff of Fire Gulch City.
ISBN 978-0-7614-5962-0 (hardcover) —
ISBN 978-0-7614-6075-6 (ebook)
[1. Magic—Fiction. 2. Hats—Fiction. 3. West (U.S.)—Fiction.] I. Title.
PZ7.L2575To 2011 [E]—dc22 2011000031

This here is the story of Tornado Slim. It starts one fine day as Slim roused himself from an afternoon snooze. He had no idea what he was in for.

"Afternoon, pard'ner!" said a coyote.
"Afternoon," Slim said warily.

“Say, think you could do me a favor?” asked the coyote. “I’ve got this letter here fer the sheriff of Fire Gulch City. I’d deliver it myself, but it’s my weddin’ day. If I’m late, my fiancée will be right sore with me. What do you say?”

“W-well,” Slim stammered, “I uh . . .”

"Okay, okay," interrupted the coyote. "You drive a hard bargain. I admire that. Let's say I sweeten the deal a bit and give you this here hat."

"It sure is a fine-lookin' hat," said Slim, "but I . . ."

The coyote quickly pushed the letter and the hat into Slim's hands. "I sure do 'preciate it, pard'ner. Now use that hat carefully, you hear?"

Before Slim could say another word, the coyote was off.

Seeing as he had nothing better to do, Slim decided to deliver the letter.

When he finally staggered into a small town hours later, his feet felt ready to fall off.

Think I'll relax with an ice-cold sarsaparilla, he thought.

SALOO

Then Slim noticed all the commotion. Folks were scrambling about and shouting.

"Better high-tail it outta here, stranger!"

"The dam's 'bout to bust!"

WARE
BANK
DRY

Slim took off his hat and scratched his head. Then he saw it. *Of all the rotten luck!* Water was bursting through the broken dam. And Slim was right in its path!

“Oh, boy,” he muttered.

Slim closed his eyes and gritted his teeth. But after a moment he realized he was still standing. Not only that, he was bone-dry.

Slowly, he opened his eyes. The water was flowing right into the hat!

BANK
DRY GOODS

Slim heard cheering.

"Way to go, pard'ner! You done saved our town!"

The townsfolk cooked up a feast of smoked ribs, corn on the cob, plenty of baked beans, five-alarm chili, and a great, big barrel of sarsaparilla. Slim could have stayed forever, eating free food and enjoying all the attention. But then he remembered the letter in his pocket. He set out again for Fire Gulch City.

By the time he reached the next town, Slim's legs felt ready to come loose.

Whew, boy, **he thought, entering a saloon.** ***Sure could go for an ice-cold sarsaparilla.***

But before he could bless the barstool with his behind, he heard a shout.

"Twister!"

Everybody began to panic. Everybody except Slim; he had the hat.

"Back in a moment, folks," he said, sauntering outside.

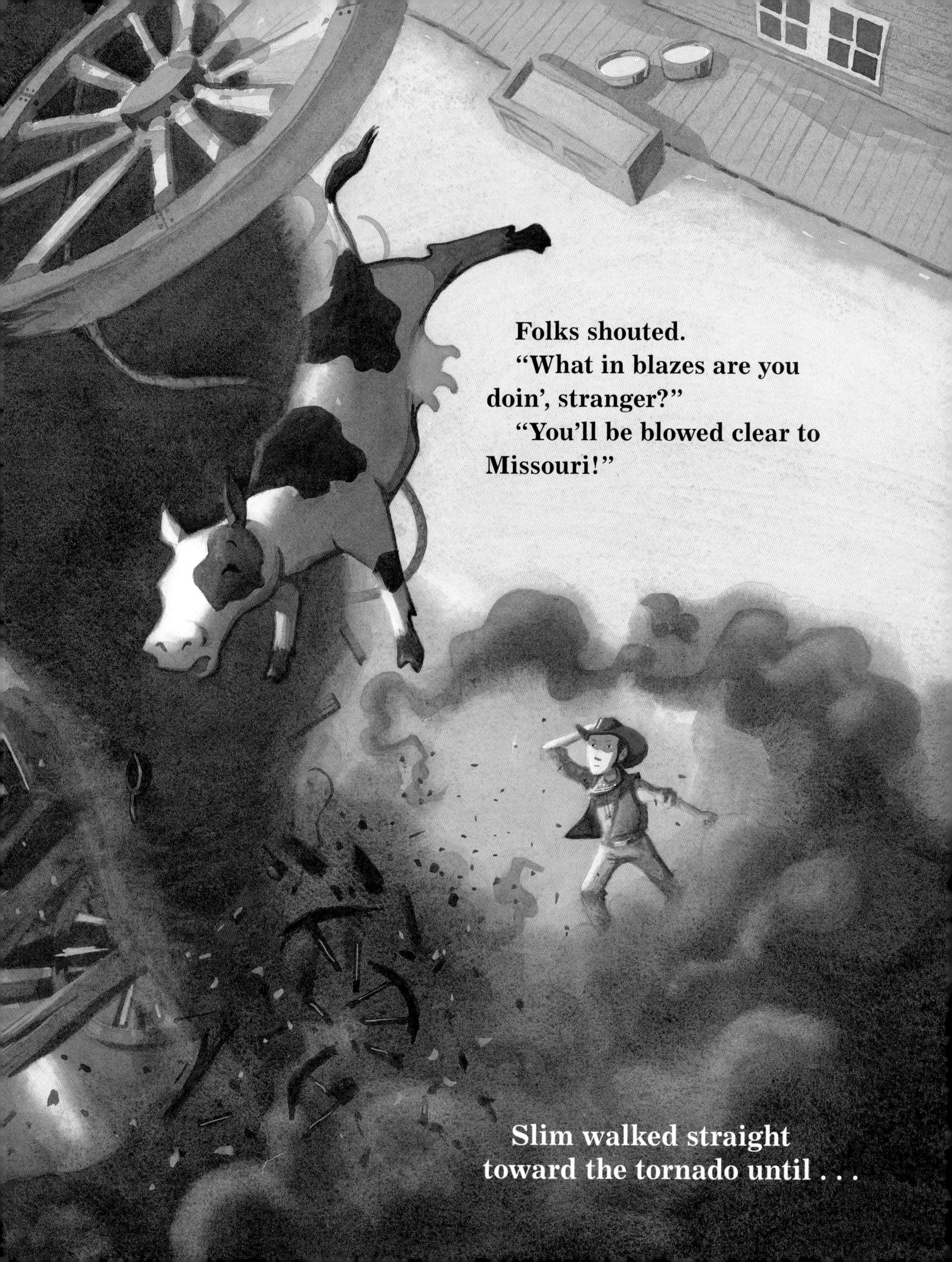

Folks shouted.

"What in blazes are you doin', stranger?"

"You'll be blowed clear to Missouri!"

Slim walked straight toward the tornado until . . .

Whoosh! He spun around and around something awful, faster and higher each time.

Dizzier than he'd ever been in his whole life, Slim grabbed the hat off his head.

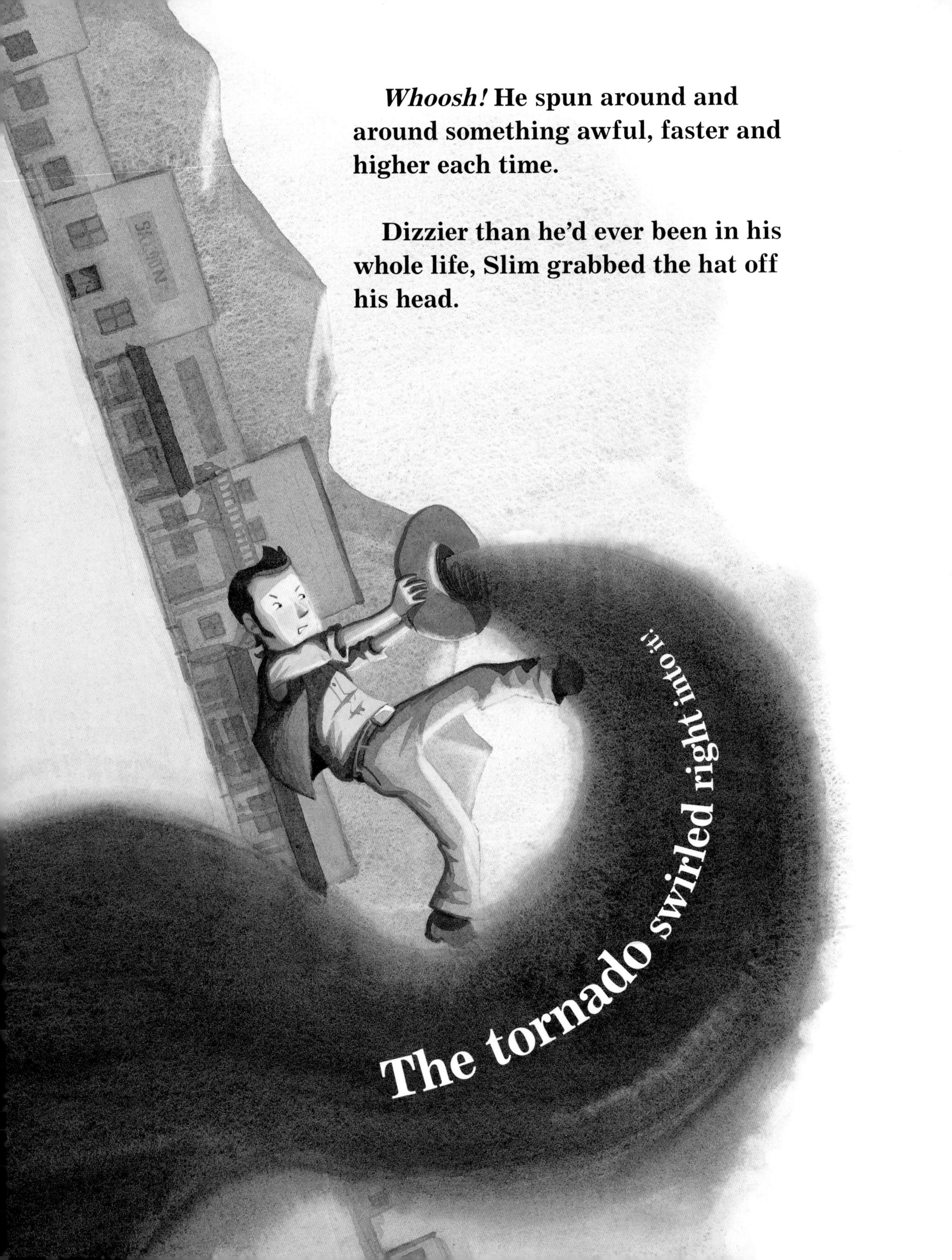

The tornado swirled right into it!

Now on solid ground, Slim put the hat back on.

Folks cheered.

"You saved our town!"

"That fella done took on a tornader!"

Another barbecue was prepared. There were smoked ribs, corn on the cob, plenty of baked beans, *six*-alarm chili this time, and a great, big barrel of sarsaparilla. Slim didn't stay too long, though. He had to get to Fire Gulch City. The coyote was counting on him.

By the time Slim reached the next town, his whole body felt ready to crumble. But once again, the ice-cold sarsaparilla would have to wait because . . .

BANK
HANK'S

"The meetin' hall's on fire!" someone shouted.

Hot dang! Everywhere I go there's some kind of disaster, thought Slim as he ran toward the burning building.

He held out the hat.

This time, all the water from the dam gushed out until the fire was nothing but a few wisps of smoke. Slim could hear the familiar sounds of folks cheering.

M. Ke

Then there was a scream.
"It's Smelly Jim!"
While everyone was distracted by the fire, Smelly Jim and his Band of Outlaws had robbed the bank! They were headed for their getaway wagon.
"Halt!" shouted Slim.

Esq.

He had nearly caught up to the bandits when a gust of wind blew the hat off his head. The hat did a twirl through the air and landed right at Smelly Jim's feet!

“Thanks, pard’ner,” laughed Smelly Jim. As he lowered the hat onto his head, the hat began to tremble.

“I wouldn’t do that if I were you,” Slim warned him.

Before you could say *sarsaparilla*, the tornado shot out! Smelly Jim and his Band of Outlaws were whisked into the air. ’Round and ’round they went. Their cries could barely be heard over the roar of the wind.

"I'm gonna be sick!"
"I want my mommy!"

The hat flew out of Smelly Jim's hand and headed right for Slim. As soon as Slim caught it, the tornado swirled back into it.

The street was quiet. Smelly Jim lay facedown in the water trough. Sprawled out around him was his Band of Outlaws.

The townsfolk cheered as Slim led the bank robbers to jail.

"Nicely done, pard'ner!"

"You showed 'em!"

The mayor approached Slim. "How'd you like to be sheriff of our fine town?" he asked.

"Me? Sheriff?" asked Slim. "Sir, I'd be honored."

"Then you got yerself a job," said the mayor. "Now let's get that barbecue pit fired up, folks! Bart, how 'bout a batch of that seven-alarm chili of yers? We've got some celebratin' to do!"

ATTORNEY
MERCANTILE

"There's jest one thing," Slim said. "I have to go to Fire Gulch City first."

The mayor gave Slim a funny look. "Shoot, son, this here *is* Fire Gulch City!" he boomed.

"Are you kiddin'?" said Slim. "I've got a letter here fer the sheriff."

GULCH CITY JAIL

“Well, then,” said the mayor, “I reckon that there letter is fer you, ’cause yer the only sheriff we got. Last one left to get married.”

How do you like that? thought Slim. *That coyote ran me ragged, and for what? To deliver a letter to myself!*

Slim opened the letter.

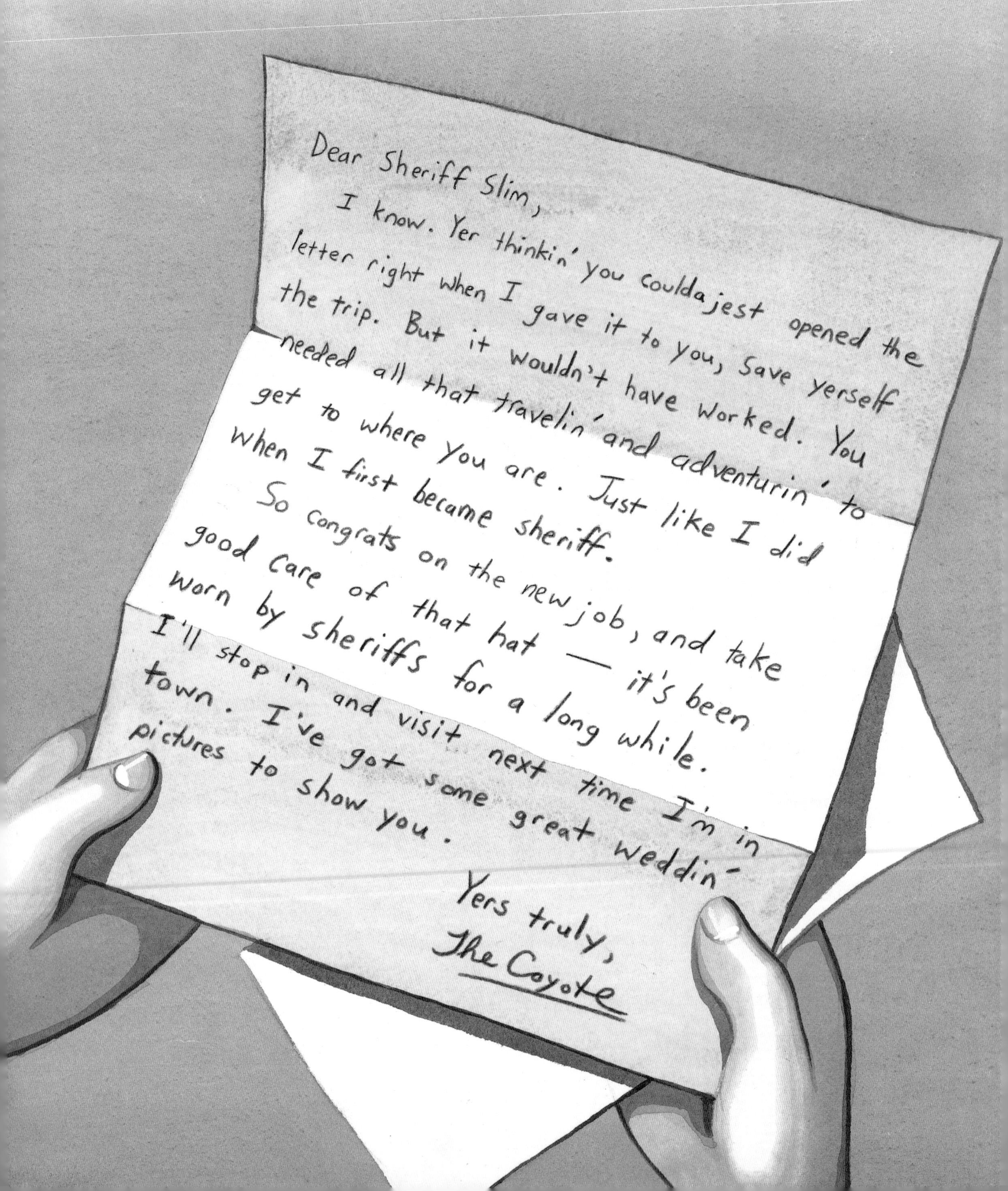
Dear Sheriff Slim,
I know. Yer thinkin' you couldajest opened the letter right when I gave it to you, Save yerself the trip. But it wouldn't have worked. You needed all that travelin' and adventurin' to get to where you are. Just like I did when I first became sheriff.
So congrats on the new job, and take good care of that hat — it's been worn by sheriffs for a long while.
I'll stop in and visit next time I'm in town. I've got some great weddin' pictures to show you.
Yers truly,
The Coyote

A Picture's Worth 1,000 Words

A Picture's Worth 1,000 Words

A Workbook for Visual Communications

Jean Westcott & Jennifer Hammond Landau

JOSSEY-BASS/PFEIFFER
A Wiley Company
www.pfeiffer.com

Published by

JOSSEY-BASS/PFEIFFER
A Wiley Company
989 Market Street
San Francisco, CA 94103-1741
415.433.1740; Fax 415.433.0499
800.274.4434; Fax 800.569.0443

www.pfeiffer.com

ISBN: 0-7879-0352-3
Library of Congress Catalog Card Number 96-077826

Printing 10 9 8 7 6

We at Jossey-Bass strive to use the most environmentally sensitive paper stocks available to us. Our publications are printed on acid-free recycled stock whenever possible, and our paper always meets or exceeds minimum GPO and EPA requirements.

Acknowledgments

We wish to thank all of the people who have been a part of creating this workbook.

In particular we would like to acknowledge David Sibbet, Mary Gelinas, Tom Sherman, and Ed Gibbons. David's pioneering creativity and dedication to growing graphic facilitation capability within colleagues and organizations has been an inspiration and a guide to us in our work and in the creation of this workbook. Mary, Tom, and Ed pilot-tested the first and second drafts. Their encouragement and specific, detailed feedback was instrumental in shaping the final edition.

To the many colleagues and workshop participants who encouraged us to put our approaches to paper and who tested our exercises, we offer heartfelt appreciation. We hope in reading this workbook that you will recognize your many ideas and the influence of your suggestions.

TABLE of CONTENTS

Part I: Basic Skills Practice

Part II: Applications

INTRODUCTION

A picture is worth a thousand words. We like pictures and know their power. Pictures have power because they can be understood with minimal time or effort, they're efficient, and they communicate on an intuitive and emotional level as well as on the cognitive level.

Although we generally understand the power of pictures, most of us are more at ease using words rather than pictures. When asked, many trainers, teachers, managers, and consultants say they are convinced that the use of visuals can increase the impact of their work. However, they also acknowledge that they rarely create and use pictures. For many the key constraint indicated is a lack of confidence in their ability to draw and a perception that drawing is something that only "artists" can do. This workbook will give you the skills and confidence to express yourself with pictures, i.e., to draw.

A Picture's Worth 1,000 Words is a resource for anyone who makes presentations to large or small groups of people. Whether you intend to educate, inform or persuade; whether you are speaking to a few people or to many; and whether the group is composed of students, staff, managers or community people, the use of simple visual images will support effective communication. Adding graphic images or pictures to your presentations will help you to:

- Become clear ahead of time about what you want to communicate.
- Capture and maintain audience attention.
- Assist your audience in understanding the information and ideas you present.
- Efficiently explain complex concepts.

- Be seen by your audience as credible and persuasive.

- Help your audience to remember what you've said.

If you're new to visual communication, this workbook will introduce you to the basic skills needed for increasing the effectiveness of your presentations. If you have experience with visual communication, the information and exercises will affirm and extend your skills. Whatever your current skill level, we encourage you to use this workbook as an opportunity to extend those skills through practice.

How this work book is arranged.

The workbook is divided into two sections: basic skills/practice and information/application. Two-thirds of the workbook is pictures (examples of graphics used in our work) and practice activities for you to complete.

In the practice part of the workbook we'll introduce you to the basic skills you will need to use felt tip markers to create flip charts and posters. Most of what is presented is also of use in preparing overheads, course materials -- hand-outs -- and for general "thinking with a pencil."

The presentation of skills reflects a developmental sequence. So we begin with what is likely to be most familiar, i.e., lettering -- how to print quickly and legibly; when to use upper and lower case letters, and, special alphabets. Then we look at how to create graphic symbols using simple shapes, e.g., squares, circles and lines. From there, you'll learn to draw multiple objects by determining the basic shape that composes that object. We continue using basic shapes to show how to draw cartoon faces, Next, you will learn special techniques to increase your ability to draw what you see. You'll learn to draw arrows, hands, and people. And finally, you'll practice designing a presentation poster.

The practice activities are drawn from those we found most successful in our graphics workshops. We've learned that people want skills that can be used immediately. And so, the basic skills practice activities can be completed in one 2-3 hour sitting (of course, you can certainly spend more time if you want to!)

Upon completion of the practice activities, you will be able to: print clear, attractive letters; use basic shapes; draw cartoon faces, hands, people, and various objects; and, design a poster. At the end of those 2-3 hours, you will have learned all of the basic skills. Then it's just a matter of using the skills as a way of continuing to develop those skills.

The second section of the workbook contains additional information that will help you apply the basic skills. You'll find information about developing graphic vocabulary, tips for recording, computer graphics, and much more. In this section we take a broad look at application, i.e., the use of graphics is not limited to an instructional or presentation focus, but is expanded to apply to meetings, problem solving, decision making, and planning. We've included examples of some of the ways we use graphics in our consulting and training.

This is simultaneously a workbook and a reference...a reusable re-source. Once the exercises are completed, you can revisit the work you've done to remind yourself how to create certain images and for specific ideas that are appropriate to each new situation.

About the authors

Jean Westcott is a management consultant whose work has a primary focus on Meeting Facilitation and Team Development. She discovered the power of pictures as a communication tool ten years ago when she attended a graphics workshop taught by David Sibbet (and co-taught by Jennifer).

Jennifer Hammond Landau began her work in organizations as a graphic facilitator and has successfully supported herself for the last ten years by drawing on the walls of hundreds of training rooms and corporate board rooms. This has allowed Jennifer to consult with clients regarding all aspects of system-wide visioning and strategic planning, project and product design, and team building.

The authors practice what they preach. For both Jean and Jennifer visual communication is an integral part of their work. Together they bring 30+ years of experience as consultants and trainers, and so, know the audience they have targeted with this workbook. And like their audience, neither has received formal training in art prior to incorporating visual communication into their work.

Both of the authors have been frequent conference presenters and course instructors in visual communications. In 1987 they collaborated in the creation and publication of *A Field Guide to Flip Charts*. This pocket-sized booklet summarizes key principles for the use of visual communication and the creation of flip charts for presentation posters. *A Picture is Worth a Thousand Words* is the second product to emerge from their work and teaching.

We hope you find the information and exercises to be simple, practical and fun. To let us know what you think, or for more information, please call either of us: Jean @ 510-536-1657; Jennifer @ 415- 255-2893.

Have Fun!

LETTERING

Making a presentation visual begins with the "word pictures" that we already have available, i.e., the letters of the Alphabet.

Many presentations can be enhanced simply by the addition of a single flip chart which states in clear, BOLD letters the title or theme of the presentation.

For EXAMPLE:

She who
LAUGHS
...lasts!

AGENDA
• Staffing
• Schedules
• Contracts
• In-Service

Lettering TIPS

- For headlines it's OK to use all Upper case letters when the headline is less than four words.
- Combine Upper and Lower case letters for text.
- Print quickly and boldly (adds "life" to your letters).
- Words will look best if all letters are the same height and have the same slant.
- Focus on legibility not style.
- Draw attention to a key word or phrase with a highlight (color, size or letter style).
- Avoid cute or complex lettering!

PRACTICE: Use the space below to practice printing upper case and lower case letters.

UPPER CASE LETTERS:

A B C D E F G H I J K L M N
O P Q R S T U V W X Y Z

A			B			C			D			E		
F			G			H			I			J		
K			L			M			N			O		
P			Q			R			S			T		
U			V			W			X		Y		Z	

LOWER CASE LETTERS:

a b c d e f g h i j k l m n
o p q r s t u v w x y z

a			b			c			d			e		
f			g			h			i			j		
k			l			m			n			o		
p			q			r			s			t		
u			v			w			x		y		z	

Most of the time it is best to rely on the type of lettering you were just practicing. However, when you want to draw the reader's attention, e.g. with a Title or Headline, a variety of lettering styles are available.

For example: **AGENDA**

To create these Built up letters begin with the basic upper case letter. The next step is to build up a 3-4 times heavier line on the left side of the original letter. Then add the "feet" or serifs. (The trick is to make the built-up area twice as heavy as you think it should be.)

A B C D E

F G H I J

K L M N O

P Q R S T

U V W X Y Z

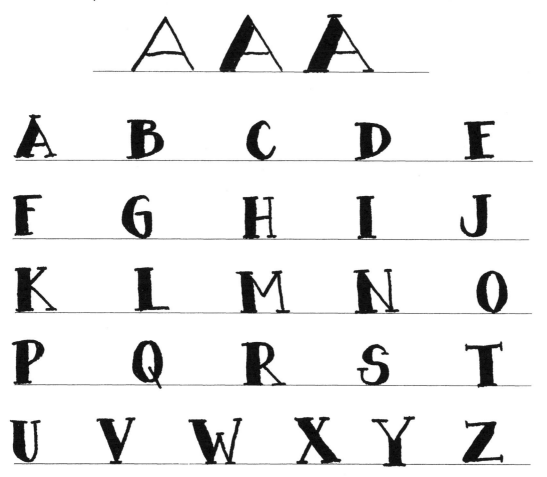

Use Built-up letters to print your first name

A second type style that we use frequently for headlines is Balloon lettering.

AGENDA

Balloon letters also start with the basic upper case letter (use a pencil). The second step is to trace around the letter to create the balloon effect. (TIP: Make the letters twice as puffy as you think they ought to be.) Once the balloon letter is completed, erase the original (pencil) letter.

A A A

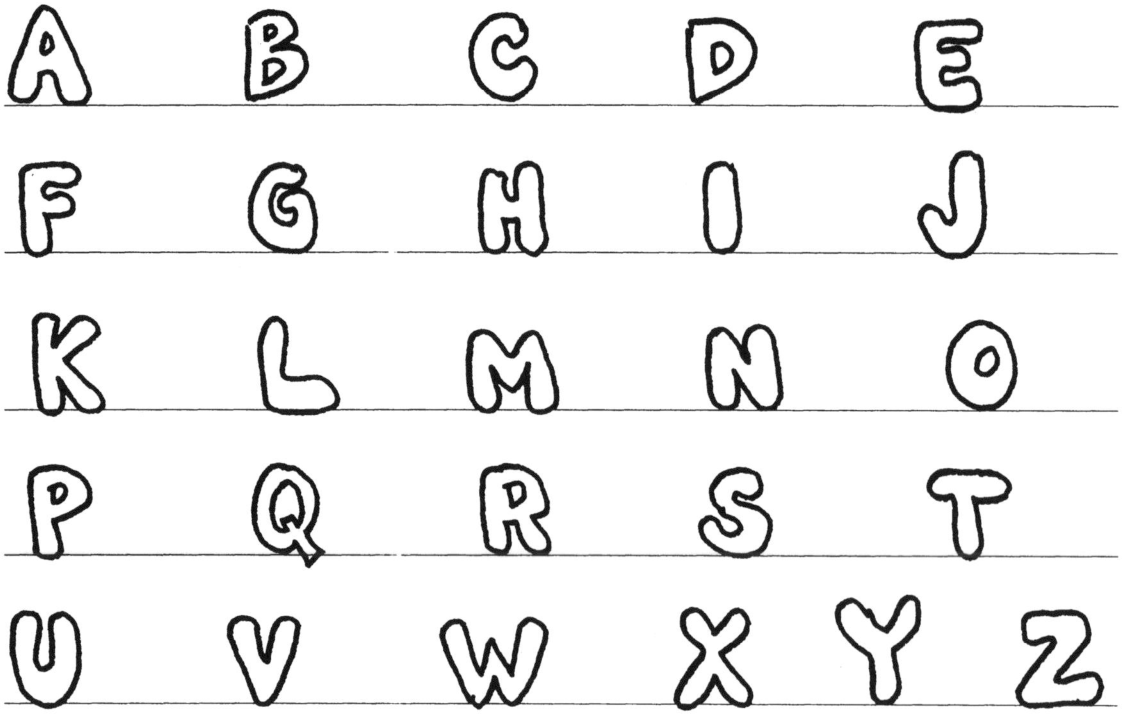
A B C D E
F G H I J
K L M N O
P Q R S T
U V W X Y Z

Use Balloon letters to print your first name

____

BASIC SHAPES

The use of basic shapes 

offers a simple, powerful way of making your message visual. Here are some ways we've used shapes to express ideas:

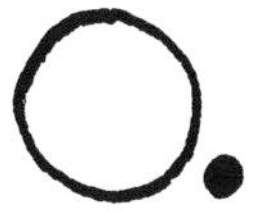

Isolation

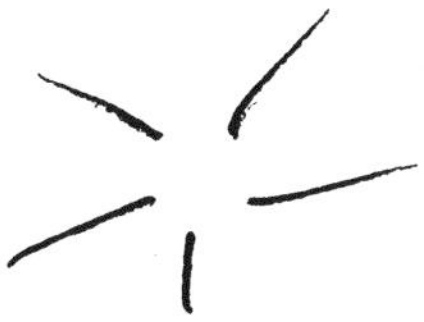

Energy

Alignment

Note: These are symbols, rather than pictures of a real object or a face.

Practice: Use the basic shapes to create a Symbol or Image for: the words CONFLICT and OBSTACLE.

Experiment...First try out several possibilities. When you have one you like, make a copy in the smaller boxes.

CONFLICT

OBSTACLE

Everything in our environment is composed of basic shapes(with seemingly infinite variation on those shapes). A key to drawing objects is being able to see the primary shape(s) that are part of that object.

Let's look at some of the thousands of things that have a circle as the basic shape:

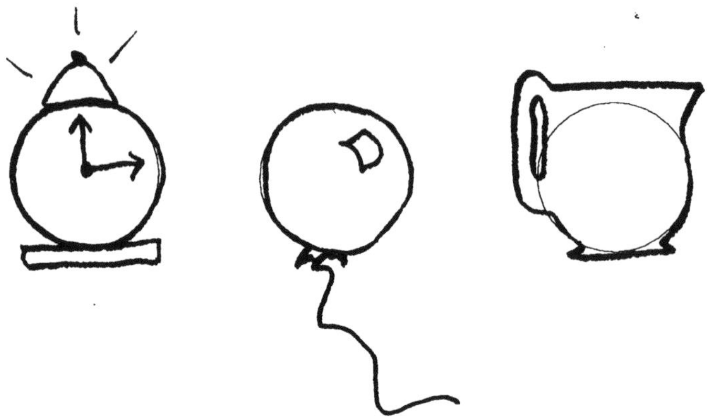

Notice that the clock and the balloon use the circle shape as is, while the pitcher has a circle as a starting place for an object that is created around the circle.

Other shapes and objects

BASIC SHAPES

Use the circles and squares to create objects that have a circle or square as a basic element. On a first try draw 2-3 circle and 2-3 square objects. In the future, when you notice other objects that use circle or square as a basic shape, add those pictures below.

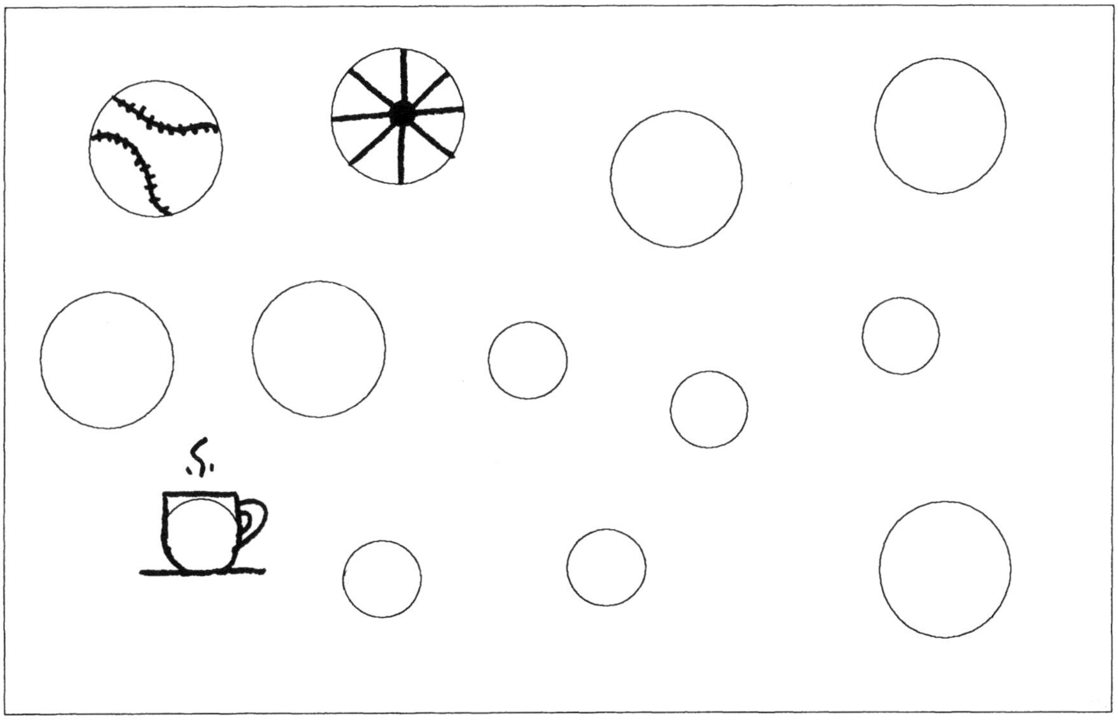

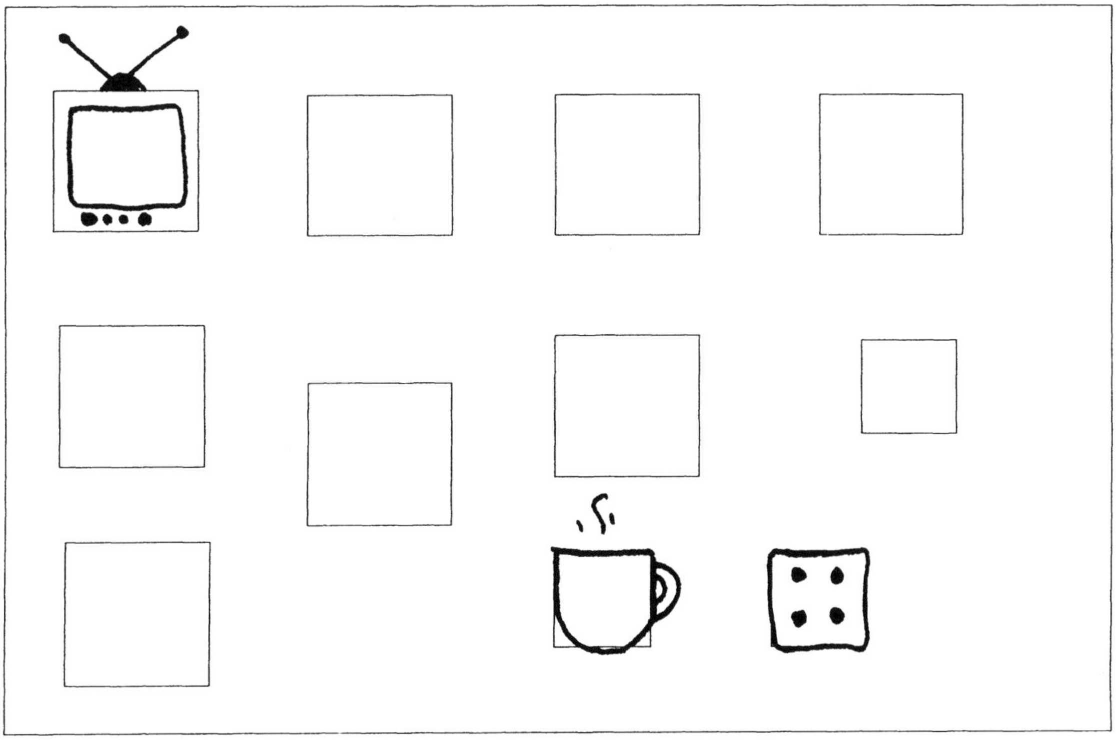

Now draw a few objects that use rectangles or polygons as a basic shape.

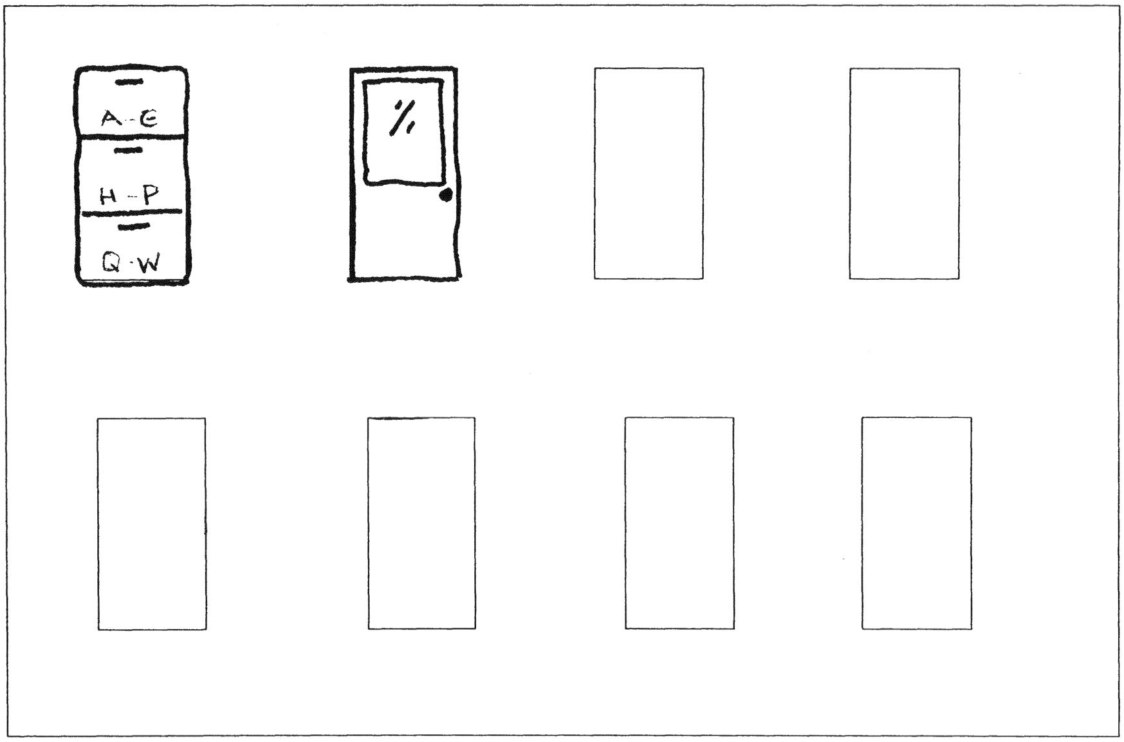
A-E
H-P
Q-W

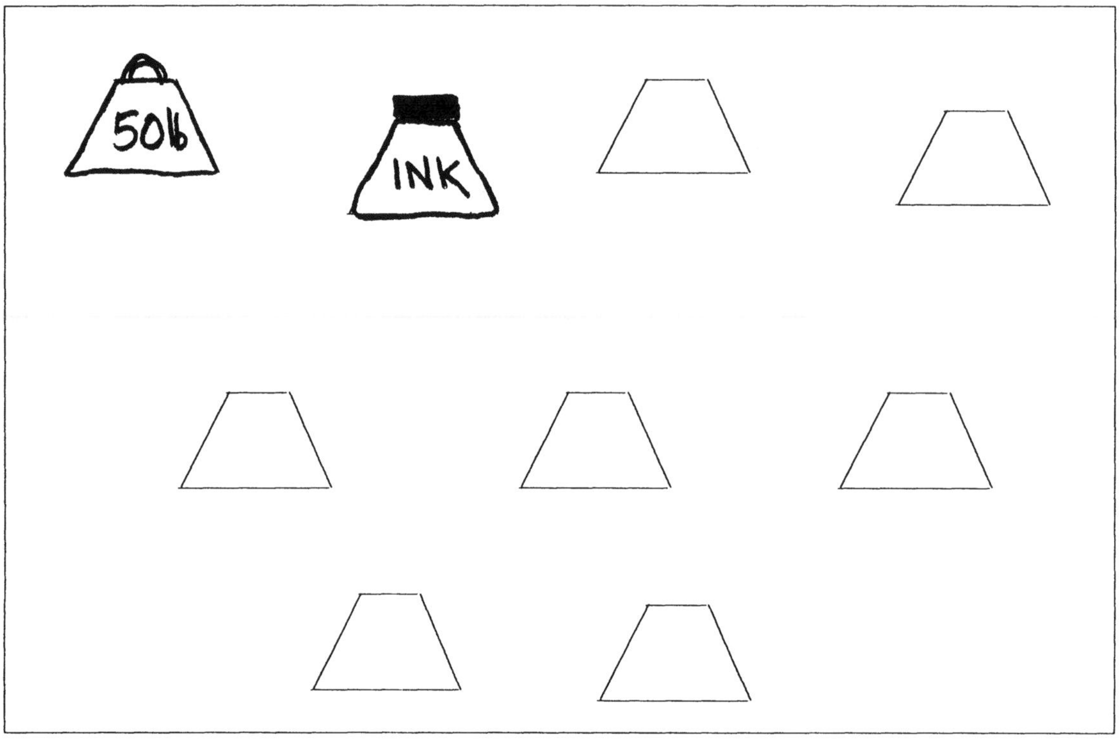
50lb
INK

CARTOON FACES

Here's another use of the circle shape. Drawing a circle is the first step in drawing the Basic Face.

A key concept in visual communication is "less is more." Applied to cartoon faces that means: only using two simple lines or dots (close together) to suggest eyes; leaving out the nose (noses don't add any expression to the Basic Face).

Use this space and follow the steps to create a basic face.

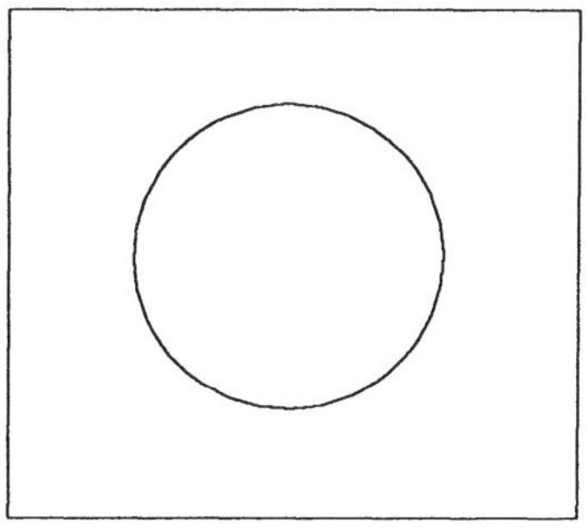

#1

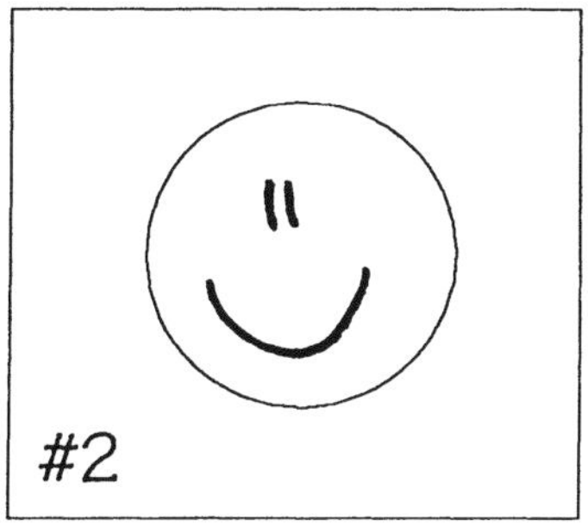
#2

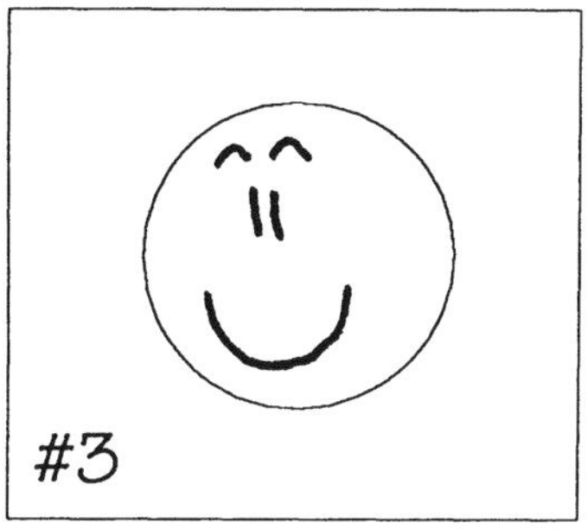
#3

To continue with some other expressive possibilities for the Basic Face.... Each of the faces below changes its' expression by variations in the placement and direction of eyebrows and mouth. Copy each of the faces a couple of times and add them to your graphic vocabulary.

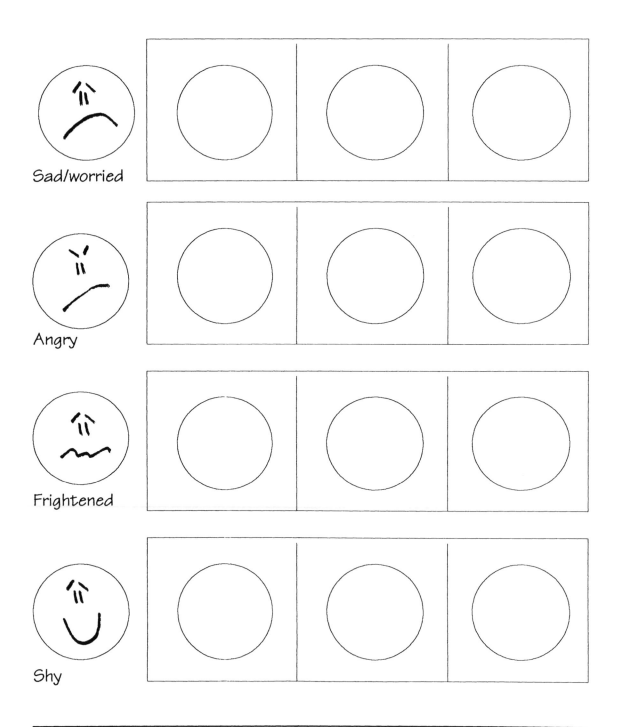

Sad/worried

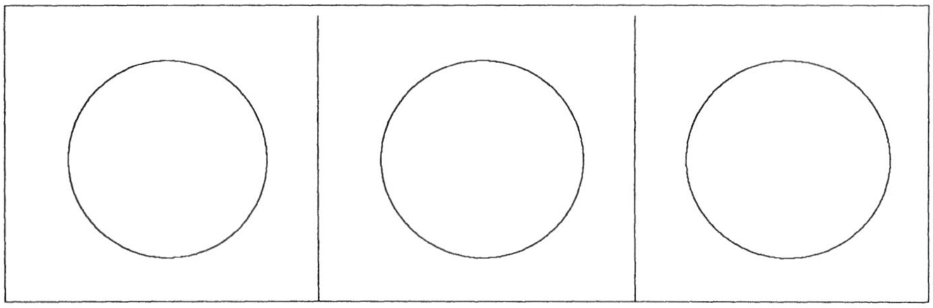

Angry

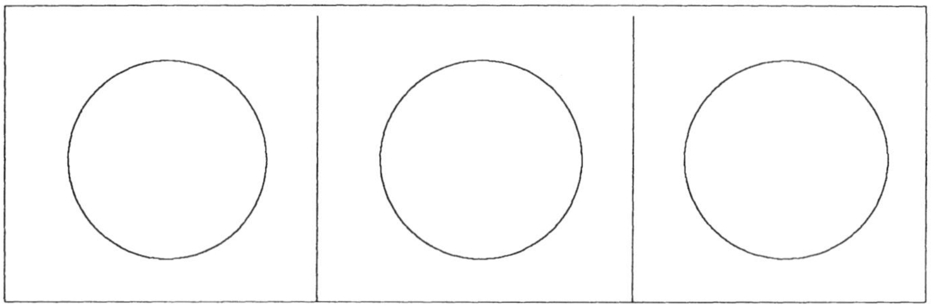

Frightened

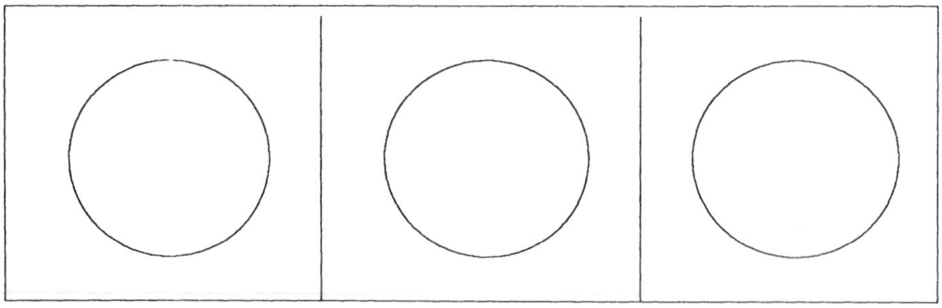

Shy

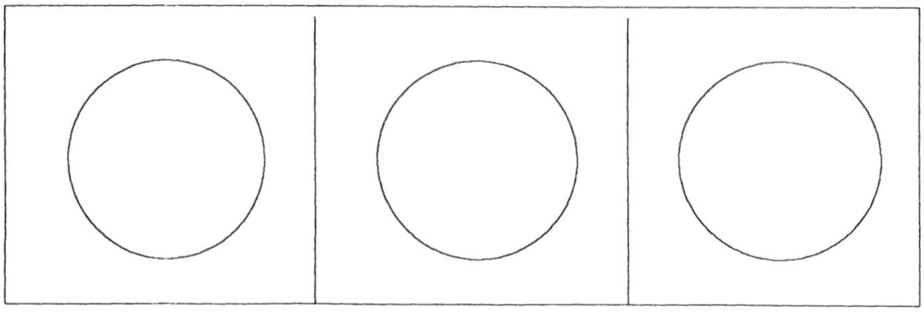

Now that you've mastered the Basic Face, let's look at a simple way of adding further expression to a cartoon face.

What we've done on this face is use ovals or circles for the eyes. This allows us to vary facial expression by adding eyelids and varying the placement of the eyeballs.

#1
#2
#3

Use this space to create the face above...follow the steps.

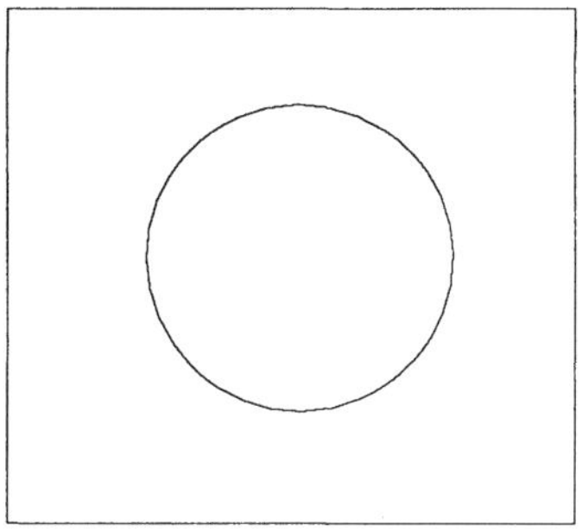

Here are more faces with oval eyes. Copy each of the faces a couple of times and add them to your graphic vocabulary.

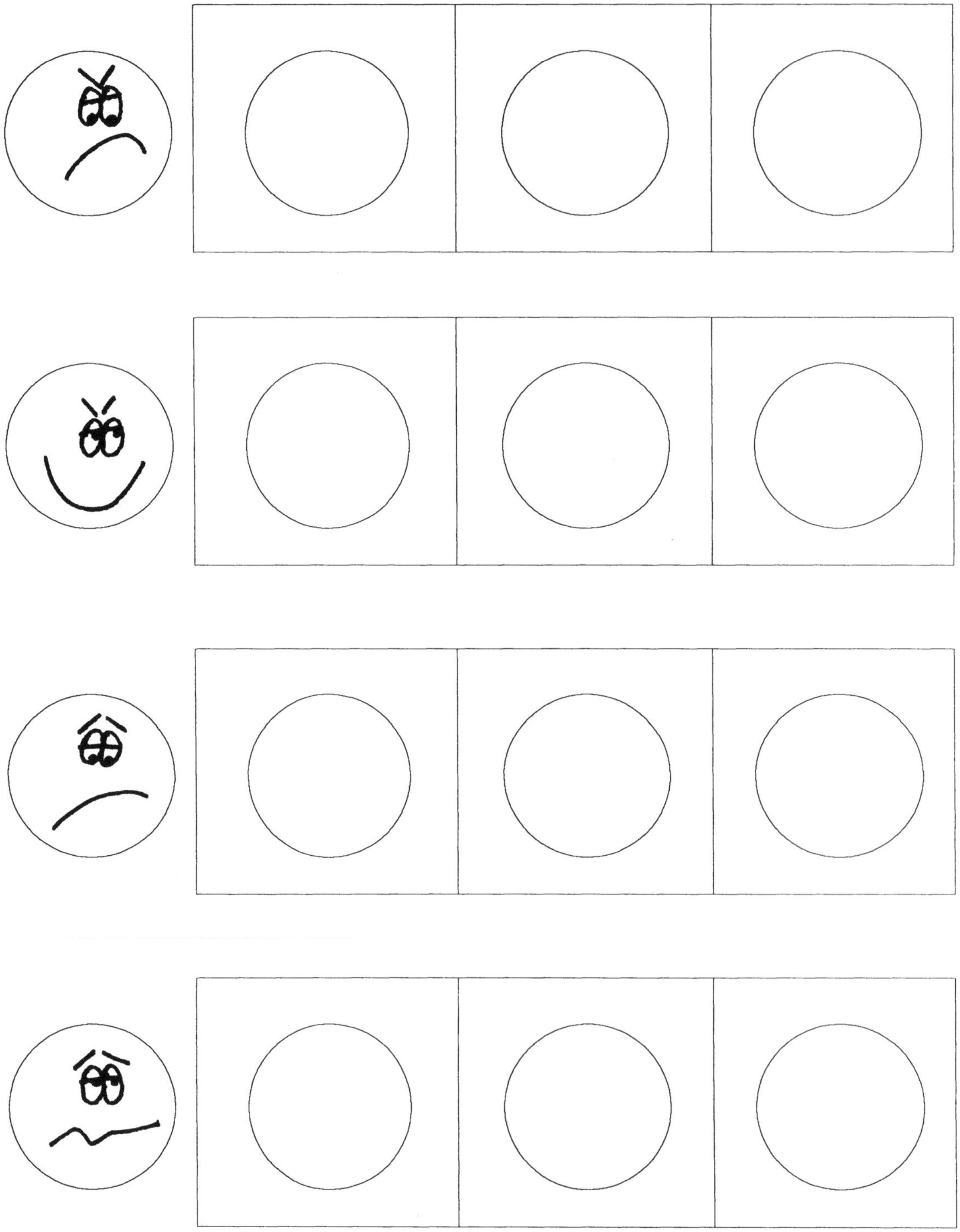

DRAWING is SEEING

Drawing is seeing. The primary difference between "artists " and non-artists" is that artists have greater access to the right side of their brain (Betty Edwards, *Drawing on the Right Side of the Brain*). The left side of the brain is our analylitical and linear side - the side that labels and judges. The right side is the intuitive side - the side that sees shapes and relationships.

Stop reading for a few minutes and complete
the practice exercise below.

Practice : Draw what you see. Using the right hand border of the box draw a mirror or reverse image of the image on the left side of the box.

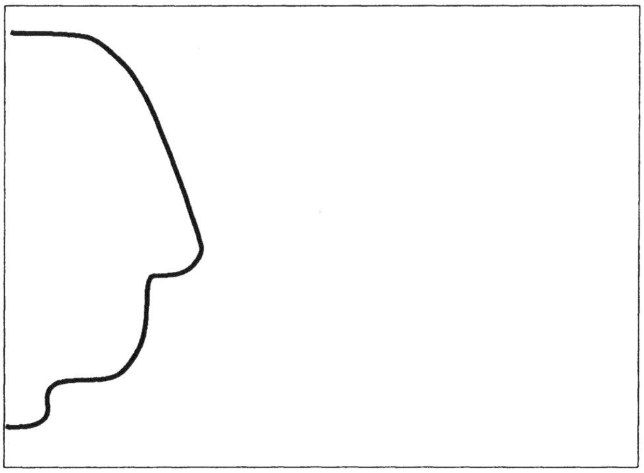

Were you able to create the mirror image with accuracy? If yes, you were probably using the right side of your brain. If no, the left side was at work. Did you "see" the shape as a person's head? If you did, this may have limited your success in accurately copying the drawing. The left side of our brain wants to figure out what the shape is, while the right side knows that labelling will prevent SEEING. The right side looks closely at lines, direction, shapes, and curves.

Something else that limits our ability to draw what we want is that we tend to look in the wrong place. Most of us spend 20% of our time looking at the original and 80% of our time looking at the drawing we are creating. Drawing is seeing. Your drawing will look more like the original if you spend most of your drawing time looking at the original!

TRY AGAIN! If your drawing is not an accurate reflection of the original, use the second practice box to try again. This time spend most of your time (80%)looking closely at the length and direction of the lines in the original shape.

Here's a chance to practice "drawing is seeing." The next two pages are examples of some of the graphic vocabulary or symbols that we use frequently (look for many more in the Graphic Vocabulary section). Copy each of the symbols at least one time. Start slowly, i.e., looking closely at the original. As you feel more confident, draw the images more quickly.

House

Tree

Cloud

Computer

The images on the preceding page are **Pictographs**. Pictographs are simple line drawings of a real object. The images below are **Ideographs,** i.e., symbols or drawings that represent an idea or abstraction. Pictographs can become Ideographs, e.g., when we decide to let a light bulb represent "idea". Some ideographs (for instance a light bulb used to represent "idea") are familiar, others you will need to borrow or create (see the Graphic Vocabulary section later in this workbook).

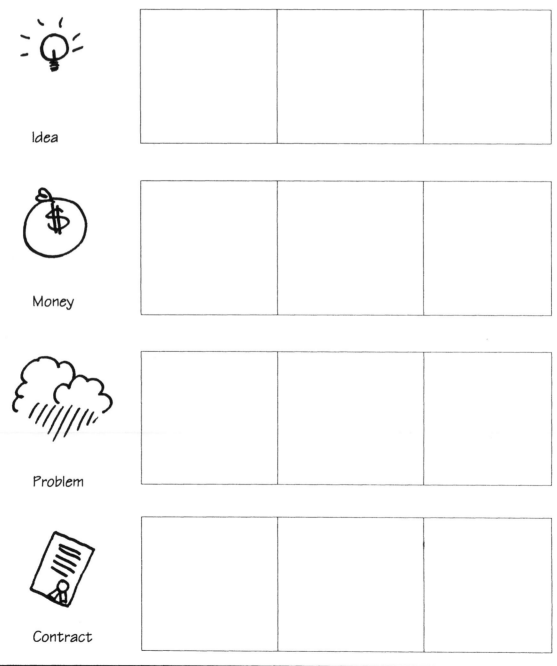

Idea

Money

Problem

Contract

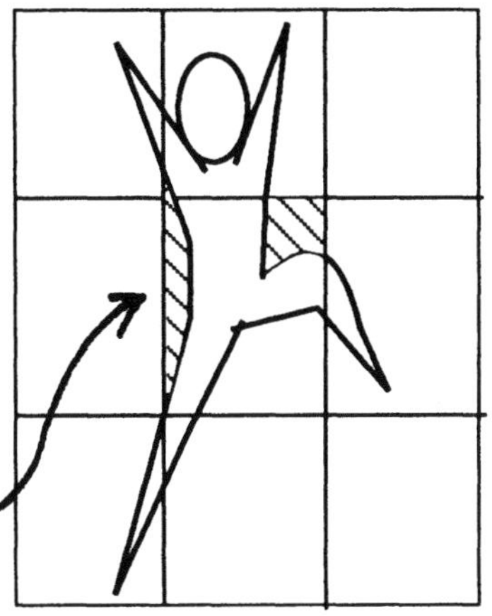

The use of a grid such as the one below can simplify the task of copying a drawing, i.e., help you to see. Use the grid below to copy and enlarge the picture on the right.

TIP: Try drawing one box at a time; look at the shapes created by "white space" in each box.

If your drawing doesn't look like the original: look closely at the individual boxes of the original drawing and your drawing; use another color of pencil to make any needed revisions.

Some other Drawing Tips

There are many short cuts for drawing. A couple that we've learned are:

• When you see a drawing/ cartoon figure that you want to enlarge and put on a flip chart.....

- Create an overhead transparency copy of the original drawing.
- Post a blank flip chart page on the wall.
- Project the transparency image onto the wall/flip chart.
- Trace the drawing onto the flip chart.

• Look for magazines that have lots of people pictures (*People Magazine* is a good example). Keep a supply of these magazines handy. When you want to draw a picture of a person engaged in an activity, e.g., talking on the telephone, eating, etc.,....

- Look for a magazine photo of that activity.
- Trace the outline or contour lines of the person/ activity in the photograph.
- Put the magazine away and add whatever detail you want to the drawing.

ARROWS

Arrows are a versatile symbol which can be used to direct attention and to visually express a range of concepts. For example:

Obstacle

Planning cycles

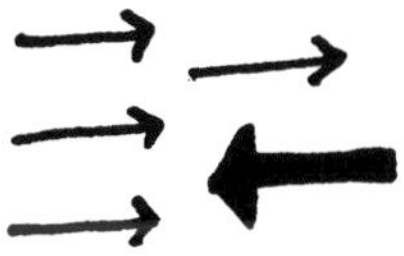

Non-conformity

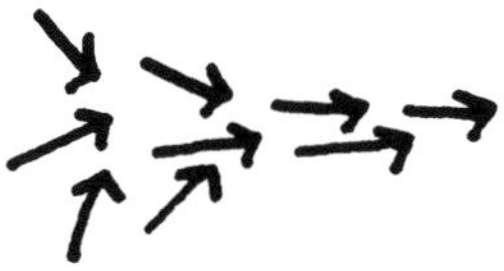

Alignment

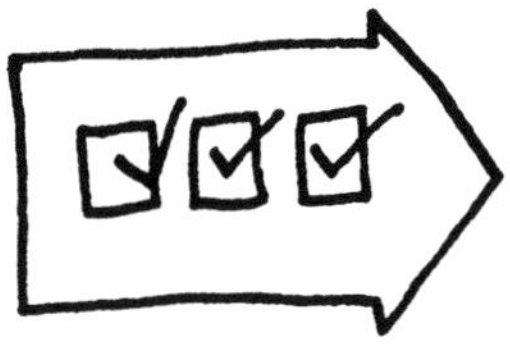

Planning stages

$

Growth

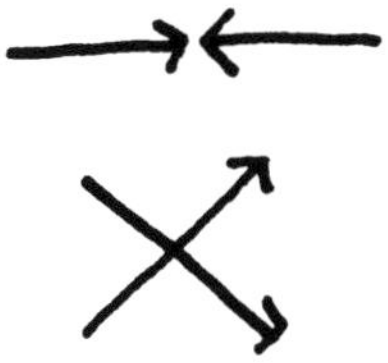

Conflict

Outreach

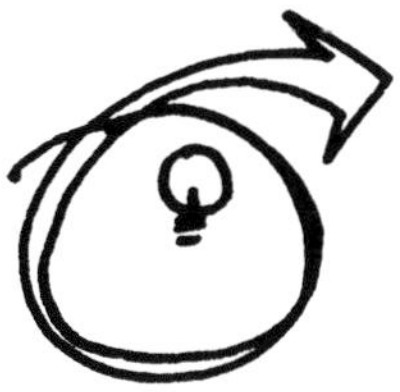

Evaluation

ARROWS

Hollow arrows are particularly useful as they can be filled with words, pictures, and color. Before you begin drawing a hollow arrow, let's look closely, let's really **see** what you'll be drawing.

Notice that the hollow arrow is actually a combination of two basic shapes -- a square and a triangle.

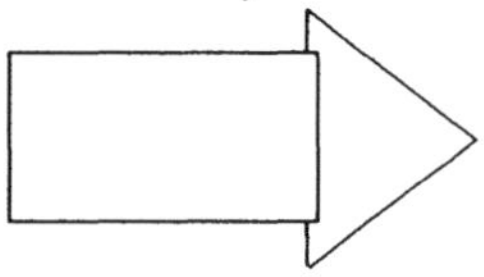

Tip: for the best looking arrows, make the "flaps" of the arrowhead smaller than the shaft.

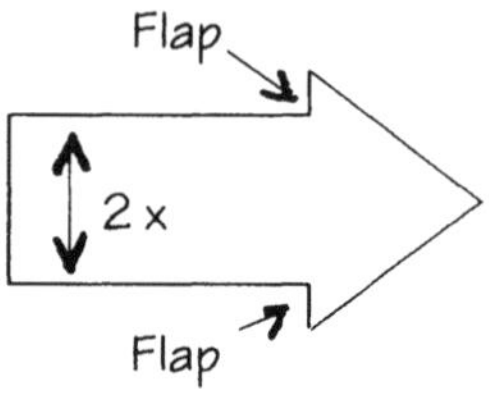
Flap
2 x
Flap

Try the following sequence as you draw hollow arrows for the first few times.

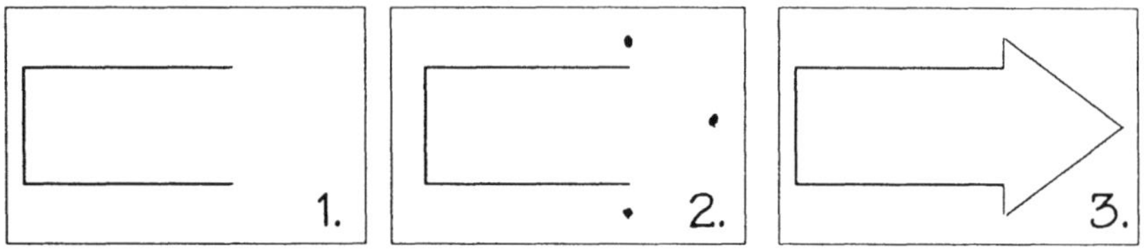
1.
2.
3.

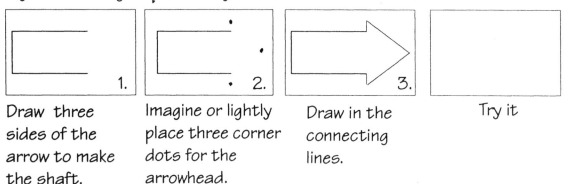

Draw three sides of the arrow to make the shaft.	Imagine or lightly place three corner dots for the arrowhead.	Draw in the connecting lines.	Try it

Practice: Hollow arrows. Once you are comfortable with this basic sequence -- try drawing the arrow in one continuous motion.

ARROWS

Hollow arrows can:

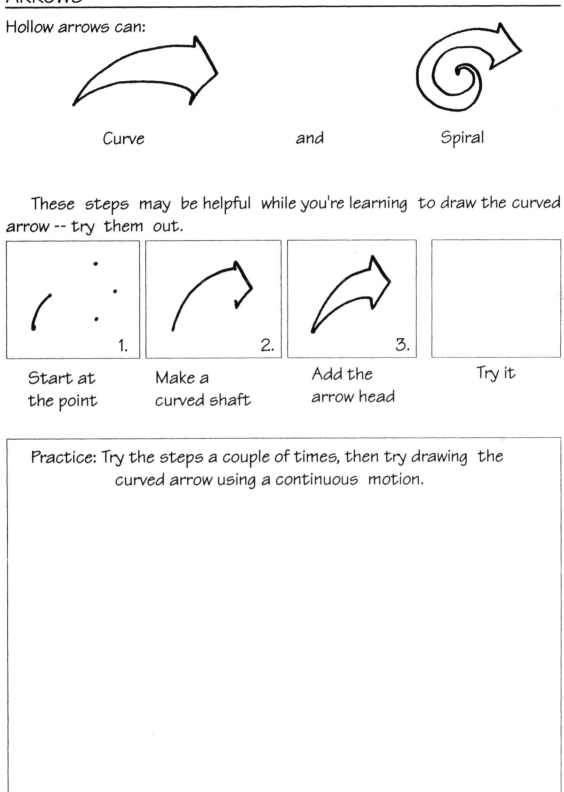

Curve and Spiral

These steps may be helpful while you're learning to draw the curved arrow -- try them out.

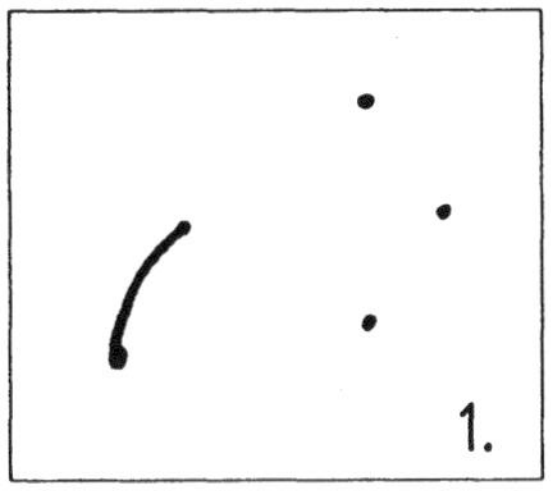
1.

Start at the point

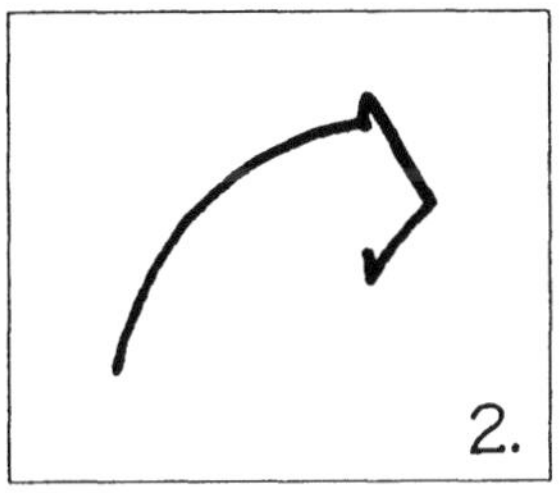
2.

Make a curved shaft

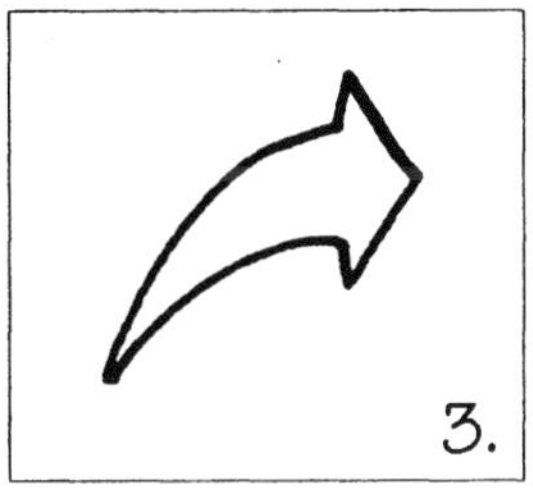
3.

Add the arrow head

Try it

Practice: Try the steps a couple of times, then try drawing the curved arrow using a continuous motion.

The spiral arrow follows the same approach

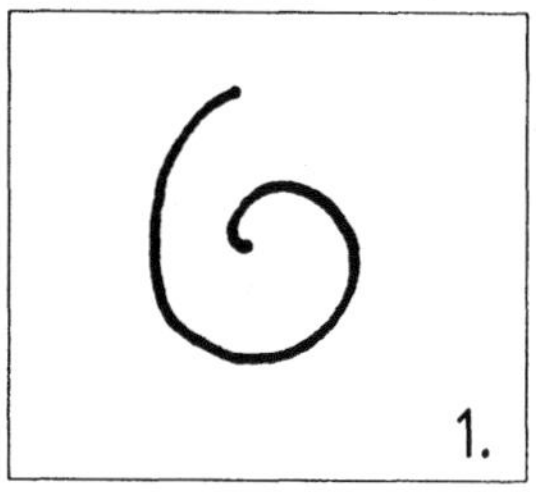
1.

Start in the middle and spiral outward

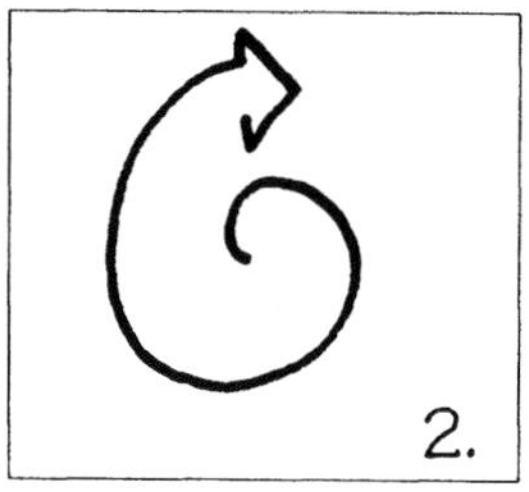
2.

Add the arrow head

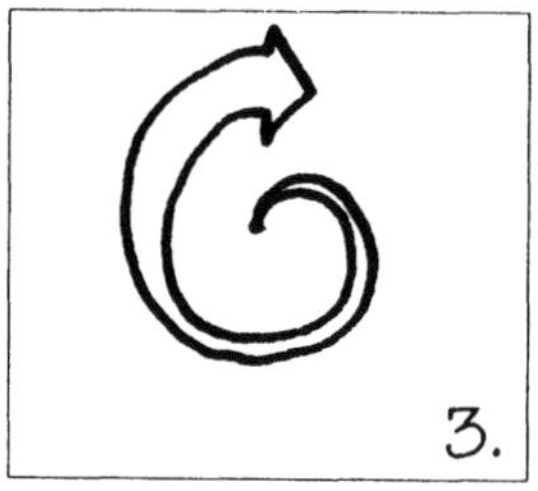
3.

And follow the spiral back to center

Try it

Practice: Draw several spiral arrows...experiment with different sizes.

ARROWS

A multi-headed arrow is built around an imaginary circle.

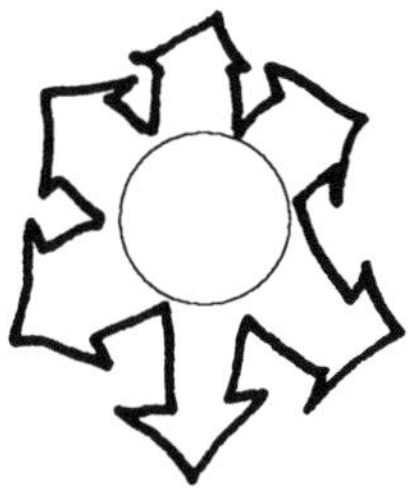

or

or

This one takes practice!

Try a couple now....come back and practice more of them later. When you feel ready, draw without the circle guide.

Below are two templates that make use of hollow arrows. Try them and invent your own.

PLANNING TEMPLATE
Current Action Items
Annual Goals
5 Year Goals
Vision Statement

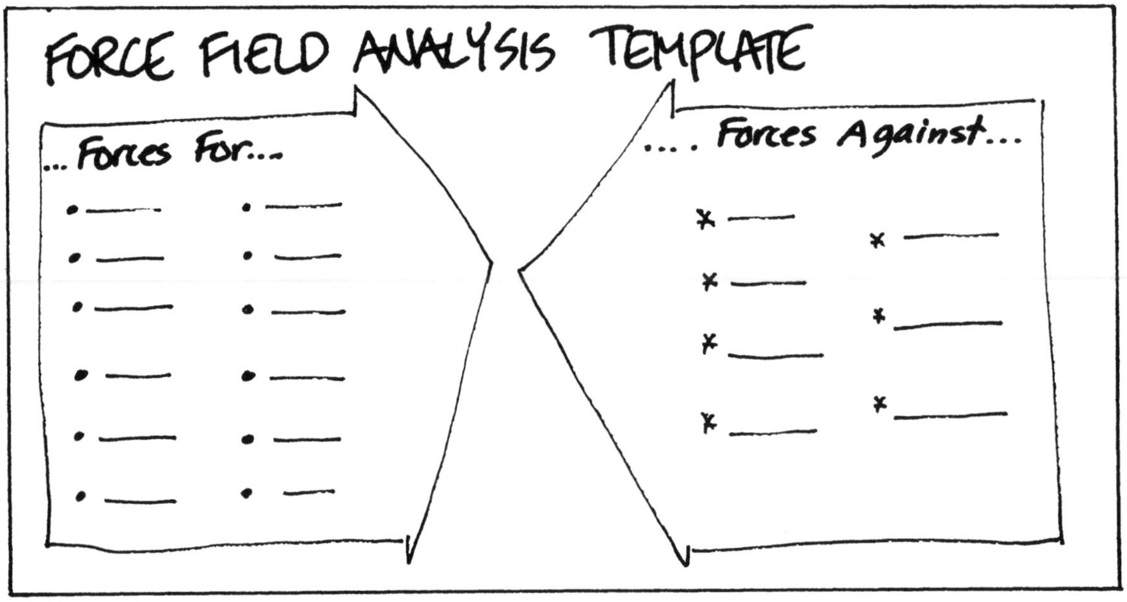
FORCE FIELD ANALYSIS TEMPLATE
...Forces For...
.... Forces Against...

DRAWING PEOPLE

Remember how to draw a simple daisy?

Drawing people is very similar! A circle with 2 "short petals" and 2 "long petals"

Practice

Practice

This can be varied... Pointed, like a star

Practice

Practice

Angular, like block letters

Practice

Practice

Rounded, like a cookie cutter

Practice

Practice

Hands and feet can be added.

Practice

Practice

Small shadow lines strengthen the effect.

Practice

Practice

Be sure the shadow lines touch the person.

...Unless you want the person to jump

Practice

Practice

TIP: Usually we don't add faces to these simple people.
Once again, less is more.

DRAWING PEOPLE

One advantage of drawing people in this way, rather than the familiar stick figure, is the flexibility. On this page and the next one are pictures of people in varied activities. Use the practice space to copy each of the people one or two times.

Pointing

Practice

Practice

Loving

Practice

Practice

Sitting

Practice

Practice

Leading

Practice

Practice

Walking

Practice

Practice

Presenting

Practice

Practice

Pushing

Practice

Practice

Groups of people can be drawn

in clusters

joined by a circle

Other details or simple drawings can be added to vary the meaning...

Try it out

Meeting

Large group
or community

Family

Teamwork

Simple perspective techniques are useful for creating groups of people.

Smaller figure
indicates distance

Overlap suggests
distance as well

Notice that figures in
the background have
less detail than figures
in the foreground

DRAWING HANDS

Most of our non-verbal expression comes from our faces and hands. In the interest of simplicity and creating a powerful visual message, try drawing just a face or a hand rather than an entire person.

Some things that hands can say.

Look Here
or Notice

Remember

Thumbs Up/
or Down

Stop

Contract
or Partnership

Holding
Something

Notice - cartoon hands can use 4 or 5 fingers;
... adding a jacket cuff adds a more finished look.

DRAWING HANDS

Practice: Draw each of the hands a couple of times. Don't forget, "Drawing is Seeing."

Look

Remember

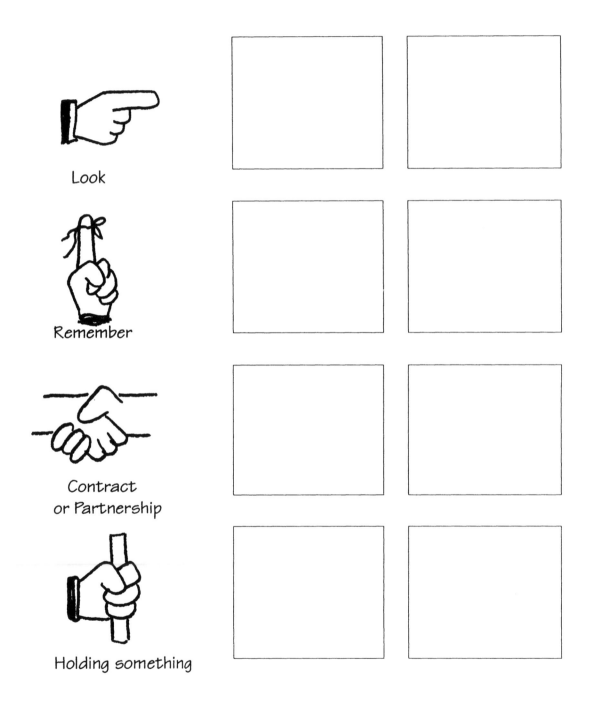

Contract
or Partnership

Holding something

POSTER DESIGN

Poster design....putting words, shapes and drawings together on a poster or page. The question to ask is, "How can I place these elements on the paper so that they capture audience attention, are easy to read, and present information clearly?"

On the next few pages we review key poster design considerations for placing text and visuals on a page.

ATTENTION

Choices about size and placement of elements on a page will direct the reader's attention. Look at the three drawings below one at a time. Notice how your eye is drawn to the boldest or heaviest element in each rectangle.

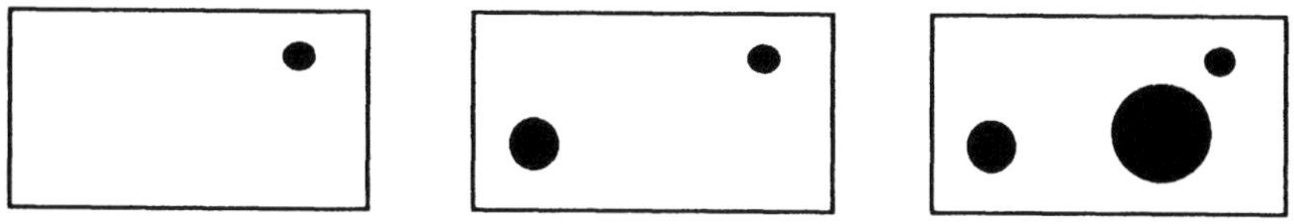

SPACE DIVISION

Unequal divisions of space are more interesting than equal divisions.

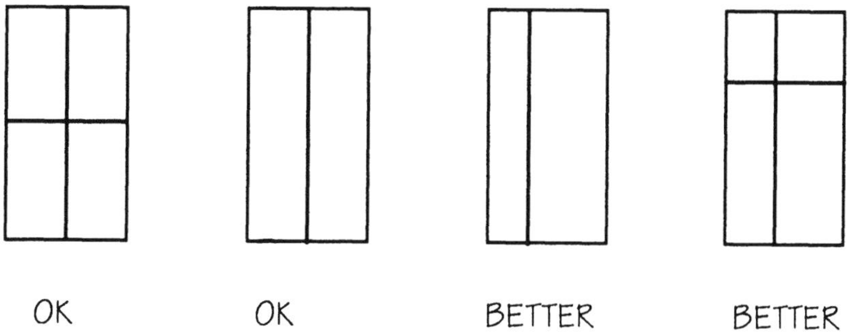
OK
OK
BETTER
BETTER

BALANCE

You should be able to draw a line down the middle of your page and feel a balance, i.e., the weight of elements on both sides of that page is approximately equal. (Big, dark and color elements "weigh" more than small, grey and white ones).

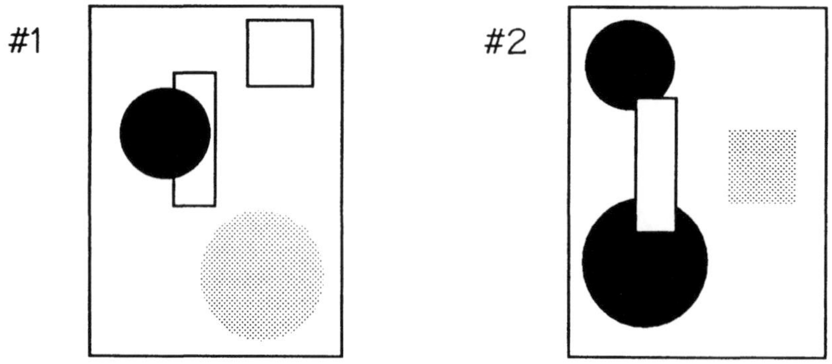
#1
#2

#1 has greater balance than #2

AVOID TANGENTIAL LINES

Two lines that cross or touch but are not intended to may create confusion for the viewer.

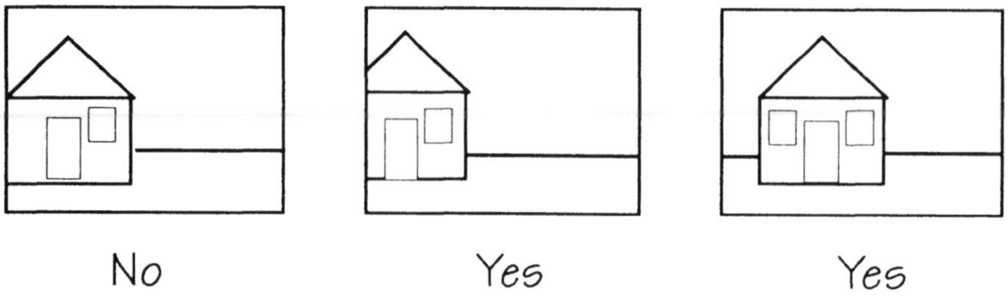
No
Yes
Yes

UNITY

Creating an appearance of a continuous flow or whole. The use of borders, arrows and overlapping text and pictures are ways to do this. Notice how the border unifies the four elements on the poster. Notice also that the poster elements and the border overlap to create even stronger unity.

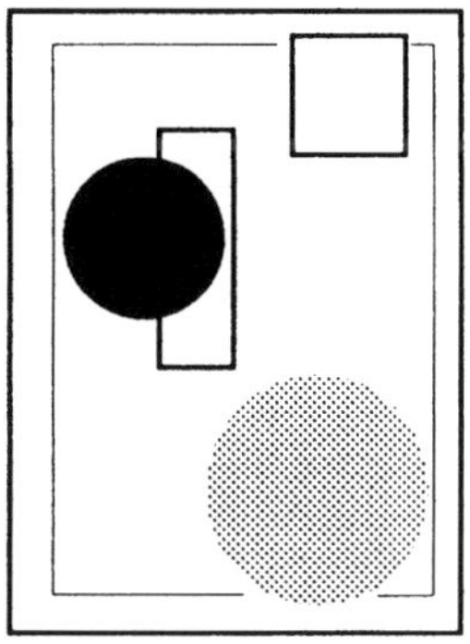

SIMPLICITY

Drawings with the fewest lines and flip charts with the fewest elements work best.

- Limit the number of lettering styles on a page.
- Create variety by varying size and density of letters.
- Colors: use at least 2, no more than 4.
- Leave lots of white ("unused") space

POSTER DESIGN

We find it very helpful to use a systematic planning process for creating posters. We try to take into account each of the design considerations described on the preceding pages. In addition, once we've chosen the words and picture(s) we plan to use, we do visual brainstorming,i.e., "thumbnail sketches". Thumbnail sketches are quick sketches or visual experiments. There's no substitute for the process of creating /seeing several experimental sketches (5-10 thumbnails may take as little as 2-3 minutes to create.) We experiment with the size of elements (text, title and picture) and their placement on the page. We need to **see** many possibilities in order to evaluate and choose the final design.

Steps for Poster Design

1. Decide what you want to say.

2. EDIT, EDIT, EDIT - Key words
   Suggestion = Maximum of 6-7 words per line;
   5-6 lines per poster page.

3. Create/ Identify visuals that support the message

4. Develop several "thumbnail sketches" to experiment with the weight, size, and placement of text and picture(s).

5. Select from "thumbnails" and create final product.

The thumbnail sketches on this page and the next were used to create a poster about Burnout. Practice your poster design skills by reviewing the thumbnai designs. Below each thumbnail sketch is space for a critique. Based on the design considerations on the preceding pages, use the space beneath the thumbnail to critique each sketch. Don't worry about correct answers (there are many). Our critiques are at the bottom of the next page.

BURNOUT

1. ______________________

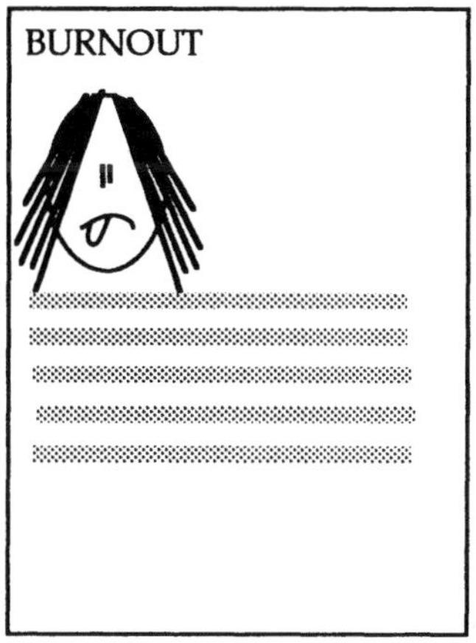
BURNOUT

2. ______________________

BURN
UT

3. ______________________

BURNOUT

4. ______________________

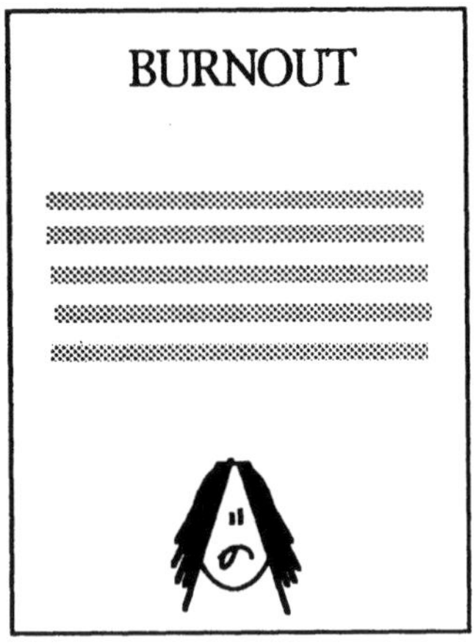
BURNOUT

5. ____________________

BURNOUT

6. ____________________

Our final choice for this poster:

BURNOUT

What "works" about this poster?

7. ____________________

1. Too much text, not much white space; 2. Lacks balance, title gets lost; 3. Use page more fully, title confusing/"cute" ; 4. Title too small..gets lost, use space more fully; 5. Three elements (title, text, picture) "float"/ no unity; 6. Not balanced.

GRAPHIC VOCABULARY

Earlier we introduced the idea of Graphic Vocabulary. Just as we have a set of words or vocabulary available for speech, it's helpful to have a graphic vocabulary. Below are some of the words or phrases we often hear used in meetings. Take a few minutes and create a picture or symbol for as many of those words/phrases as you can. (Do as many as you can before looking at the next page to see the pictures we've developed... after all, you may like yours better!)

Open-minded

Deadline

Board of Directors

Future

Bottom line

2-way communication

Budget process

Budget

Inflation
rising costs

Keynote speaker

Government

Group
Problem solving

Open-minded

July

Deadline

Board of Directors

Future

Bottom line

2-way communication

Budget process

Budget

Inflation
rising costs

Keynote speaker

Government

Group
Problem solving

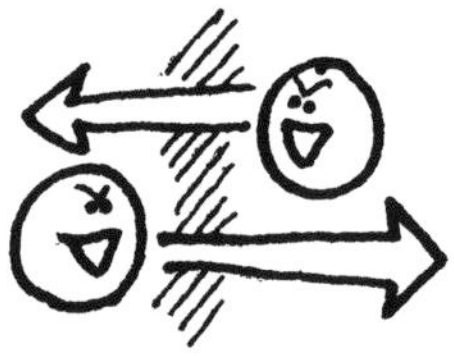

Miscommunication

Project
Vehicle

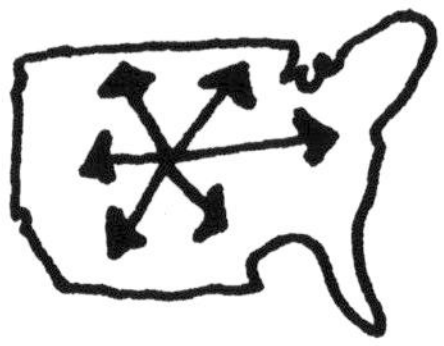

Nationwide

Congratulations!!

You have just completed the Basic Skills Practice section of this workbook. Put down your pens and pencils. This second section is for just reading. This section offers additional information that will help you apply the basic skills in many situations.

COLOR

Used judiciously color can transform a simple list into a dynamic graphic statement. Many of us make similar associations, for example: red = hot, urgent, danger ; blue = calm, water, peace; green = growth, etc. Trust your instincts about about what colors to use when. Use your own reactions when deciding which color to use when. Adopt a system of color usage which you can use quickly, comfortably and consistently.

One approach is to have "structural" or "text" colors and "highlight" colors. Given the common associations, black, brown, blue, green and purple work well for lettering, diagraming, and graphics which blend into the text. Red, orange and yellow - the "hot" colors - and purple - the "royal" color - work well as highlights. The "hot" colors tend to be harder to read in quantity and from a distance.

The objective is to make the page easy to read and attractive. Which color is often not as important as how you use the color:

- Create contrast by alternating structural colors
- Get attention and flair with small amounts of highlight
- Be subtle by using thin lines of a dark structural color, e.g. brown

GRAPHIC VOCABULARY

You had an opportunity to develop some graphic vocabulary through practice activities in the Basic Skills section. An effective vocabulary is one which comes quickly to your mind when you need it, is almost effortless to draw, and conveys immediate recognition and meaning.
Our graphic vocabulary has emerged in four ways:

#1 Using symbols that were already available.
#2 Paying attention to those fortunate or inspired moments when a graphic image pops into mind as an immediate picture/ word association.
#3 **Draw, reflect, and revise**. Sometimes we draw the first picture that comes to mind, and then we develop or refine an initial idea. (An example of that process is described below.)
#4 **Clarify concept/visual brainstorming.** when you have no ideas to begin with (process described below).

When using either the #3 Draw, Reflect, and Revise or #4 Clarify concept/ Visual Brainstorm process, we often like to work with others to create new graphic vocabulary. Working with a group of co-workers to create graphic vocabulary can be very useful (as well as creative and fun). The clarification process is often very rich as group members discover similarities and differences in how they think about important ideas, e.g., Teamwork, Quality, or Service. With frequent use your images will become part of the visual language and culture of your group or organization.

<u>TIPS for GRAPHIC VOCABULARY</u>

- REMEMBER! Your purpose is Communication (not "art")
- Less is more. Look for and draw the essence of object or idea.
- Pictures are not intended to replace words; feel free to label any graphic symbol you draw.
- There is not a universal graphic vocabulary. There's room for your creativity!
- Where there is already some agreement about the meaning of certain graphic symbols(e.g., heart = love; clock = time) use those symbols.

#3 Draw, reflect, and revise - This process is a useful one for a) clarifying an idea for yourself, and b) creating graphic vocabulary that represents your understanding of an idea or concept.
Here's an example. **CONCEPT = Teamwork**

STEP A - Draw the first picture that comes to mind when you think of "Teamwork." Here's our first idea.

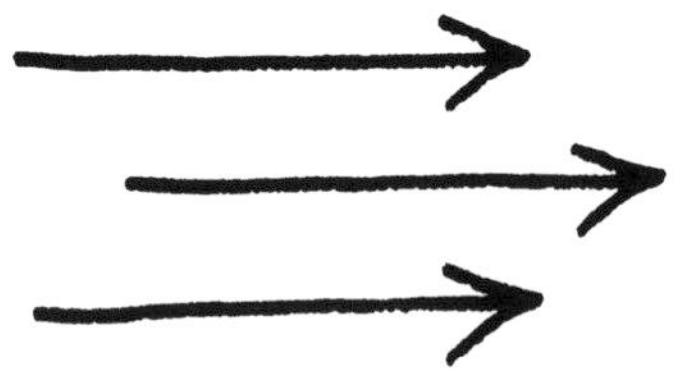

STEP B - Ask yourself, "What's wrong with this picture?" What you're asking is, "Does this picture adequately represent what this concept/ idea means for me?"

As we think about teamwork, the symbol we drew almost "works." As it is now, the image of three arrows represents one element of our idea of "teamwork', i.e., a common direction. What's missing for us? The arrows don't show the connection or relationship between people on the team.

STEP C - Revise the initial drawing to include the parts of the idea that were missing..or use the thinking you've done to try a completely different second drawing....repeat the process until you create the visual that represents your idea.

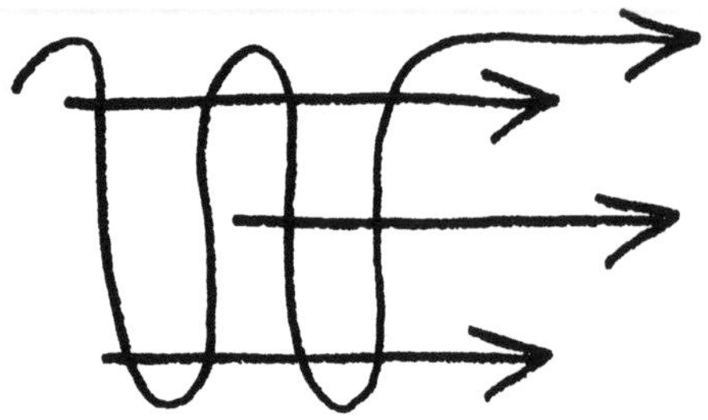

or

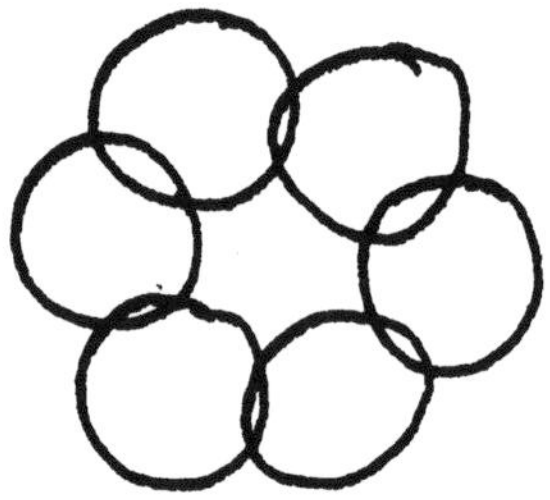

#4 Clarify concept/visual brainstorming - For all of us there are times when no pictures come to mind. Usually when we have difficulty thinking of an appropriate graphic symbol, it means that the concept we are trying to express is a complex one. What's called for is a systematic search/ creation process.

Below are the steps we use. For our example we'll continue working with the concept of Teamwork. We'll take a fresh start, as if we did not have any initial word pictures to work with.

STEP A - Define the essence of the idea - "Teamwork"

To do this we list words or phrases which express the meaning of the concept as we understand that concept.

Some words on our list:

- everyone going the same way
- shared goals, direction
- interdependence
- people together
- everyone as a resource

(don't worry if you have additional or different words)

Next we list words or phrases which are the opposite of the concept we are thinking about.

Some words on our list:

- conflicting goals
- no connections
- information witheld
- no direction

STEP B - Identify some simple pictures which represent words on your lists.

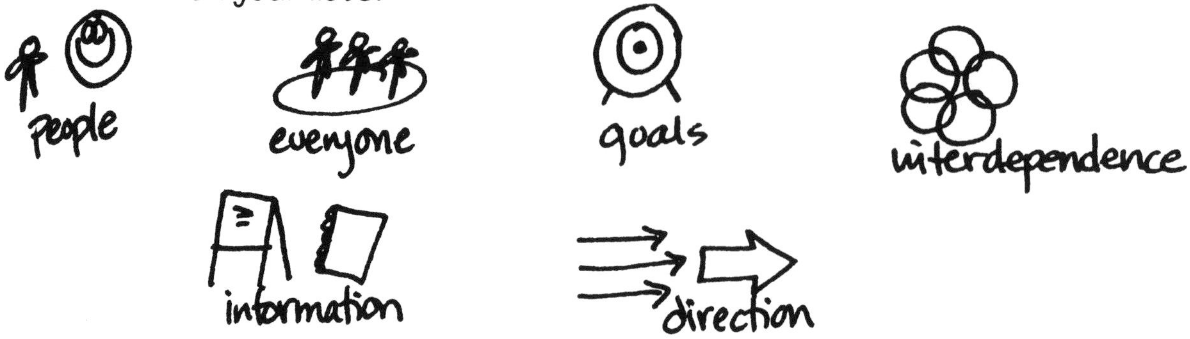
people
everyone
goals
interdependence
information
direction

STEP C - Combine visual elements. (Remember - Less is More!)

STEP D - Select, assess, refine

<u>Choosing a graphic</u> - Our decisions or choices about the final selection of a graphic image to represent an idea or word is based on several factors. We think about:

- What is easiest to draw?
- What is most quickly understood by your viewer?
- What best fits the context?
- What might have duplicate meanings?

APPLICATIONS - TALKING with PICTURES

While many presentation posters are prepared ahead of time, it's often useful to be able to "illustrate" your point as you present. Taking a few seconds in the midst of your presentation to create a quick sketch will engage your audience and help your presentation come alive! Below are some suggestions for ways to make this "spontaneous" addition of pictures effective.

TIPS for Talking with Pictures

- Stay SIMPLE and TIMELY.
  Avoid pictures and diagrams which focus attention on your EFFORTS to produce them rather that what you are EXPRESSING.

- Use KEY WORDS or VISUALS from which to AD LIB. Don't use more than 3-5 at a time, otherwise you'll spend more time trying to remember your ideas rather than developing them.

- WHEN YOU HAVE A LOT TO PRESENT.......
  Structure your thoughts into groups of ideas for which you then use 3-5 key elements per group.

- PLAN AHEAD even if your Talk is extemporaneous.
  - Have a "mental map" of how it will or might develop
  - Consider contingencies
  - Use a mini-version as your notes for self-cueing
  - If you need an intricate drawing, create the drawing in light pencil lines on the flip chart beforehand.

- Use SILENCE to build interest as you draw, i.e. Don't talk to your flip chart!

- Make your drawings large enough for the back row.

Recording - the technique of making public notes on large paper - is one of the primary applications of simple graphics and lettering. Effective recording focuses group attention on the moment, encourages better quality information, and provides an organized record for follow up. Research has shown that when ideas are posted for all to view, people judge those ideas on their value rather than by the status of the contributor. As a visual support for group and meeting process, recording externalizes information and depersonalizes input so that the data can be better analized and developed. The seasoned facilitator or presenter can use the recording to refocus the agenda and summarize progress. (If there is a lot to record, it's often helpful for the group leader to ask someone else to be a Recorder.)

Recording can take the shape of simple lists of words as is most commonly done on flip charts.

For example:

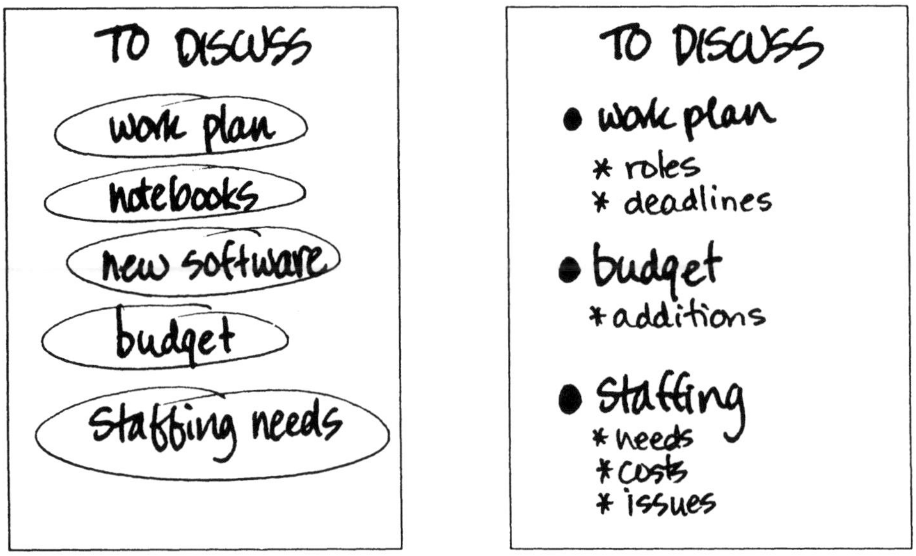
TO DISCUSS
work plan
notebooks
new software
budget
Staffing needs
TO DISCUSS
• work plan
* roles
* deadlines
• budget
* additions
• Staffing
* needs
* costs
* issues

Recording can also take a more intricate form with diagrams that connect and organize the data. Most often this requires very large sheets of paper (e.g. end rolls of newsprint)

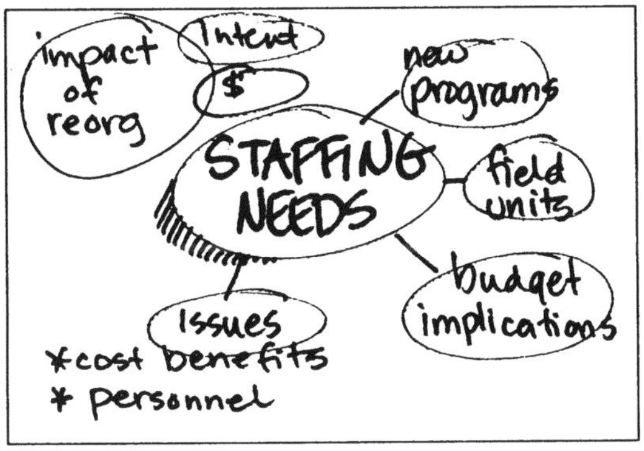
impact of reorg
Intent
$
new programs
STAFFING NEEDS
field units
budget implications
Issues
*cost benefits
* personnel

Spokes and Clusters

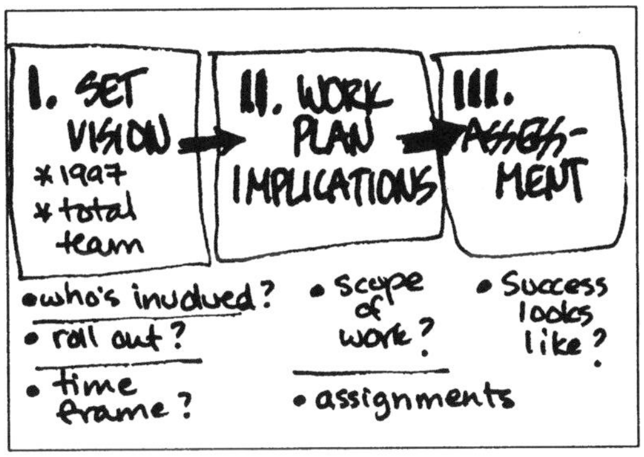
I. SET VISION
*1997
*total team
II. WORK PLAN IMPLICATIONS
III. ASSIG-MENT
•who's involved?
•roll out?
•time frame?
•scope of work?
•assignments
•Success looks like?

Flow Charts

The recording can also utilize visual themes or metaphors to stimulate thinking and to organize the data.

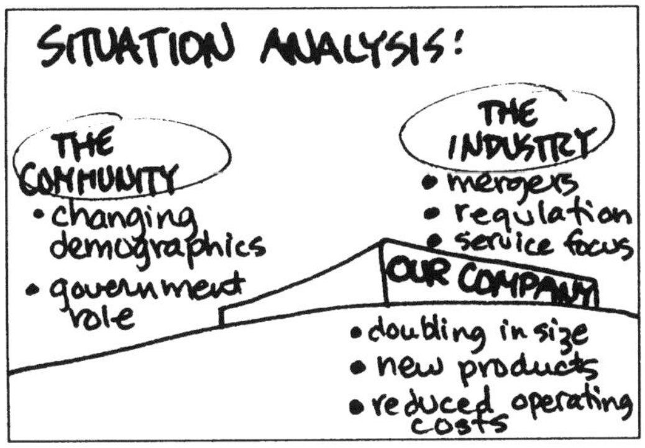
SITUATION ANALYSIS:
THE COMMUNITY
•changing demographics
•government role
THE INDUSTRY
•mergers
•regulation
•service focus
OUR COMPANY
•doubling in size
•new products
•reduced operating costs

"The Environment"

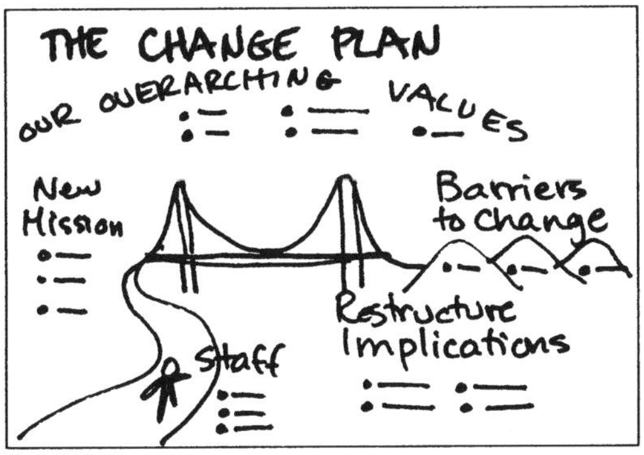
THE CHANGE PLAN
OUR OVERARCHING VALUES
New Mission
Barriers to Change
Restructure Implications
Staff

"The Journey"

GETTING STARTED:

- Plan ahead: determine the amount of paper needed and when you can change and rehang the paper.
- Arrange chairs so that the recording can be easily seen by all.
- Decide how to capture the information, i.e. outline form, flow chart, etc.

TIPS for EFFECTIVE RECORDING

- Title and number pages. Often the date is useful.

- Use bullets or color for emphasis and to differentiate the contributions of each participant.

- In general avoid numbering contributions or identifying comments with participant names (implies priority and diminishes neutrality).

- Use the speakers words: avoid paraphrasing and edit instead - carefully! Listen selectively: noun-verb-object.

- Don't upstage the meeting leader. Be sensitive to the flash of graphics and the power of the written word.

- The leader and group members' job is to assist you -ask for help if needed. Accept corrections non-defensively. Thank group members for their contributions.

- Don't be afraid of misspelling. Corrections for a final document can be done after the meeting.

- Vary the colors. Save yellow, red orange for highlighting. Follow your intuition about color choices.

- Use pictures sparingly - for quick accent, emphasis, or humor.

COMPUTERS AS A DRAWING RESOURCE

Computer graphics/ desktop publishing software is a resource for enhancing handouts and overheads. Once you have your pictures and words on the computer the production process becomes simpler and more efficient.

Numerous graphics programs are available for Macintosh and IBM. We're both Macintosh users and the programs we use most frequently are Mac Draw and SuperPaint. Those, and other Macintosh compatible software programs have easy-to-use tutorials.

The MacDraw program is a great place to start. MacDraw is an "object oriented" graphics program. As such it allows you to use what you've already learned in earlier sections about creating drawings by using basic shapes.

Below are two of the drawings we've created using this program:. These images use the Rectangle/Square, Circle, Line and Polygon tools from the MacDraw Toolbox.

TIPS for PAGE DESIGN via COMPUTER

The Poster Design suggestions reviewed earlier are still useful. Some additional guidelines:

- STYLE of TYPEFACE - e.g., Plain, Bold, Underline, Shadow. Limit your use of anything other than a Plain style. The overuse of Shadow or Outline styles is a common mistake. Limit the use of underlining; it's harder to read.

- HEADLINES -Headlines should be as short as possible and easily differentiated from body copy. The simplest ways to differentiate a headline from body copy are: Use contrasting typefaces, e.g., sans-serif (Helvetica, Avant Garde, etc., for headlines) and serif (Times Roman, Palatino. etc.) for body copy; or, use the same typeface for headline and bodycopy, but vary weights or sizes for the headline. (NOTE if the headline is more than 2-3 words, uppercase type is harder to read.)

- LESS is MORE - Resist the temptation to show off all the typefaces and style options that the computer allows. The key is restraint, e.g..few , rather than many changes, in typeface and type size.

- ALIGNMENT - the beginnings and ends of lines, e.g., flush or centered. Flush left is the most common. Centered text can be a good choice for a short headline (on long headlines, a Centered headline is harder to read).

- WHITE SPACE - Use it! White space offers the reader breathing space. The addition of white space between headline and body copy slows the reader down and can make the headline more readable

- EXPERIMENT - The goal in page design should be to improve the appearance and readibility of a page. The best design usually comes from trial-and-error. A computer makes it easy and quick to experiment with many options.

Meeting Posters. Original size: standard flip chart

MEETING OBJECTIVES
Review progress since April
Develop conference title
Determine overall format
Tour hotel facilities
Discuss plenary sessions
*Content *speakers
Meet host committee
Identify tracks
-concurrent
-mini-plenary
Develop affinity group plan

MONDAY AFTERNOON
OPENING SESSION
4:00
INTRODUCTIONS
CLARIFY HOW WE WILL WORK TOGETHER
BEGIN TO BUILD A WORKING TEAM
5:00/5:15
Evening Social Time

Graphic recording. Interactive approach to stakeholder analysis.
Original size: 4' x 6'

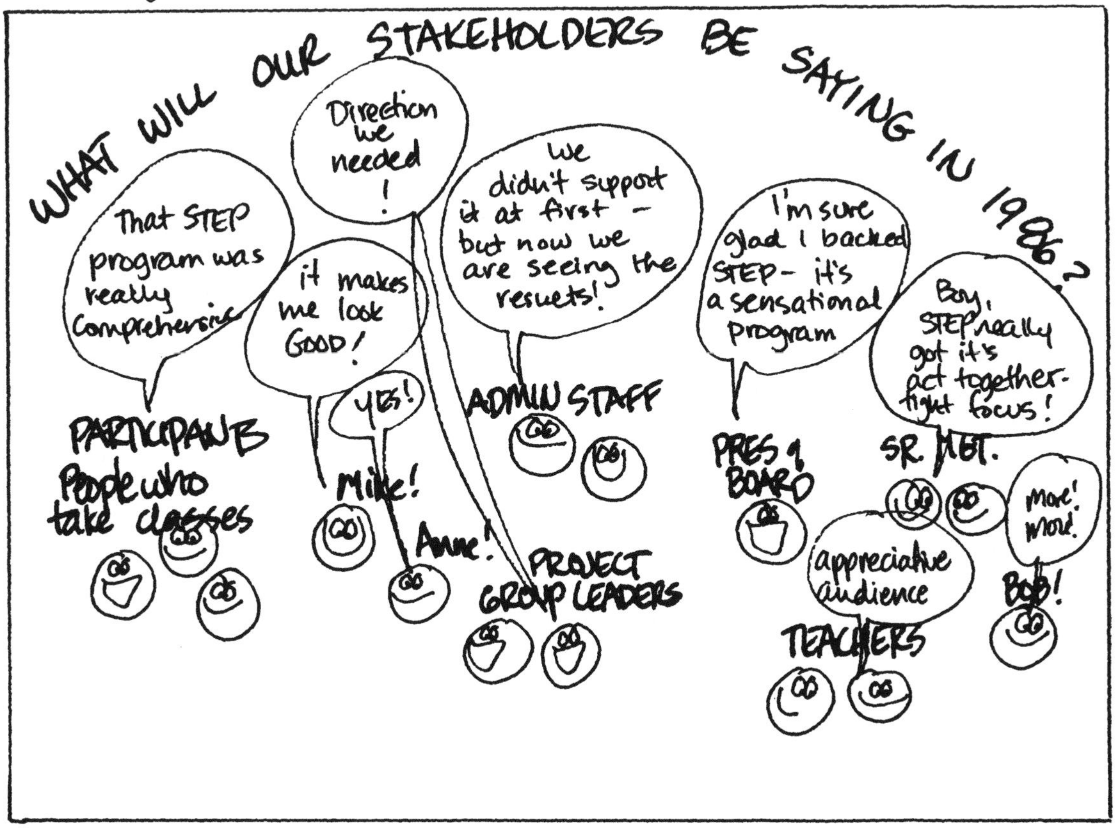
WHAT WILL OUR STAKEHOLDERS BE SAYING IN 1986?
That STEP program was really comprehensive
Direction we needed!
it makes me look GOOD!
We didn't support it at first - but now we are seeing the results!
I'm sure glad I backed STEP - it's a sensational program
Boy, STEP really got it's act together - tight focus!
YES!
PARTICIPANTS
People who take classes
Mike!
Anne!
ADMIN STAFF
PROJECT GROUP LEADERS
PRES & BOARD
SR. MGT.
appreciative audience
TEACHERS
More! More!
Bob!

Graphic recording. Embellished list style. Original size: 4' x 6'

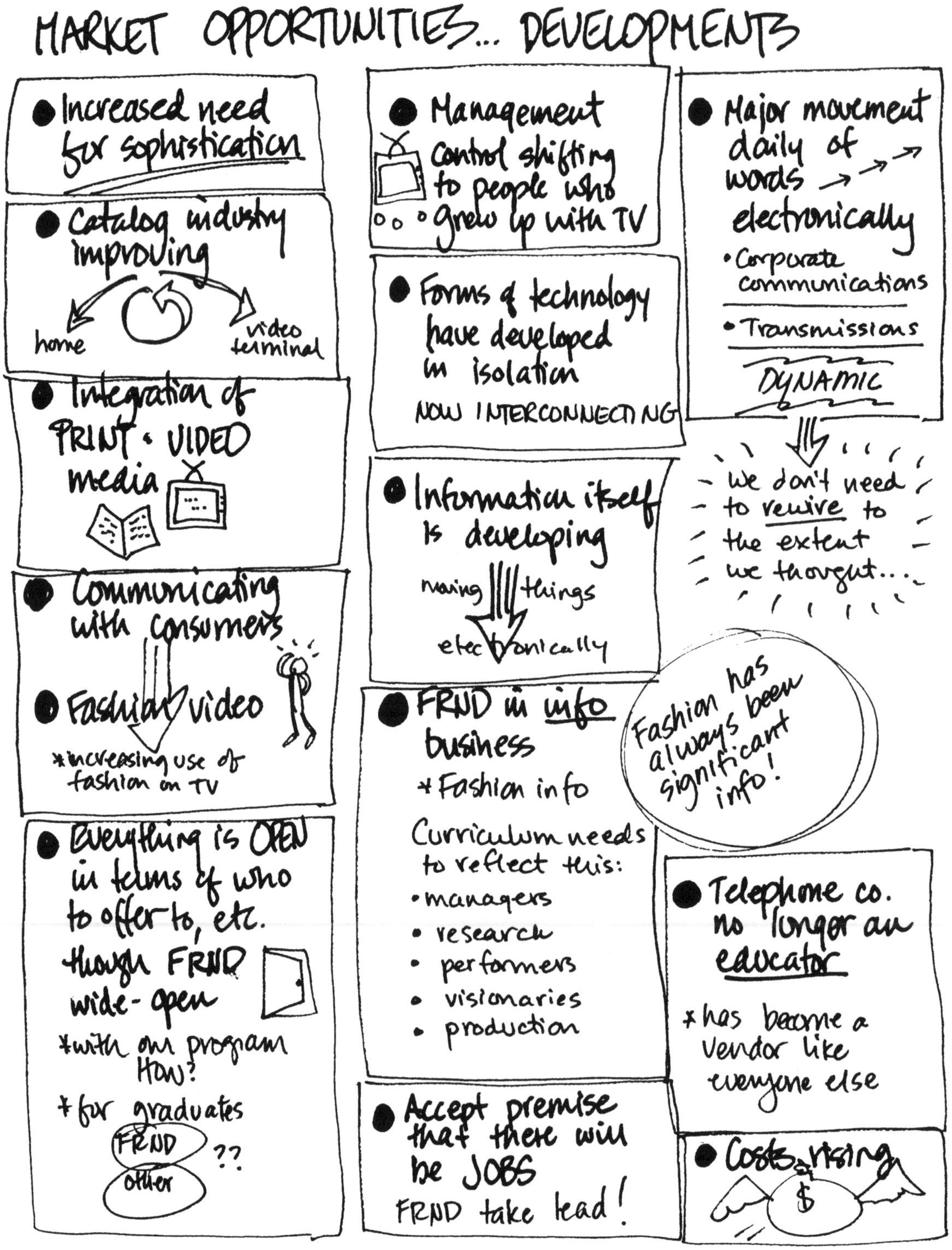
MARKET OPPORTUNITIES... DEVELOPMENTS
Increased need for sophistication
Catalog industry improving
home
video terminal
Integration of PRINT + VIDEO media
Communicating with consumers
Fashion video
*increasing use of fashion on TV
Everything is OPEN in terms of who to offer to, etc.
though FRND wide-open
*with our program HOW?
*for graduates
FRND
other
??
Management control shifting to people who grew up with TV
Forms of technology have developed in isolation
NOW INTERCONNECTING
Information itself is developing
moving things electronically
FRND in info business
*Fashion info
Curriculum needs to reflect this:
• managers
• research
• performers
• visionaries
• production
Accept premise that there will be JOBS
FRND take lead!
Major movement daily of words electronically
• Corporate communications
• Transmissions
DYNAMIC
We don't need to rewire to the extent we thought...
Fashion has always been significant info!
Telephone co. no longer an educator
*has become a vendor like everyone else
Costs rising
$

Summary Page in Project Proposal. Original Size: 8 1/2 x 11

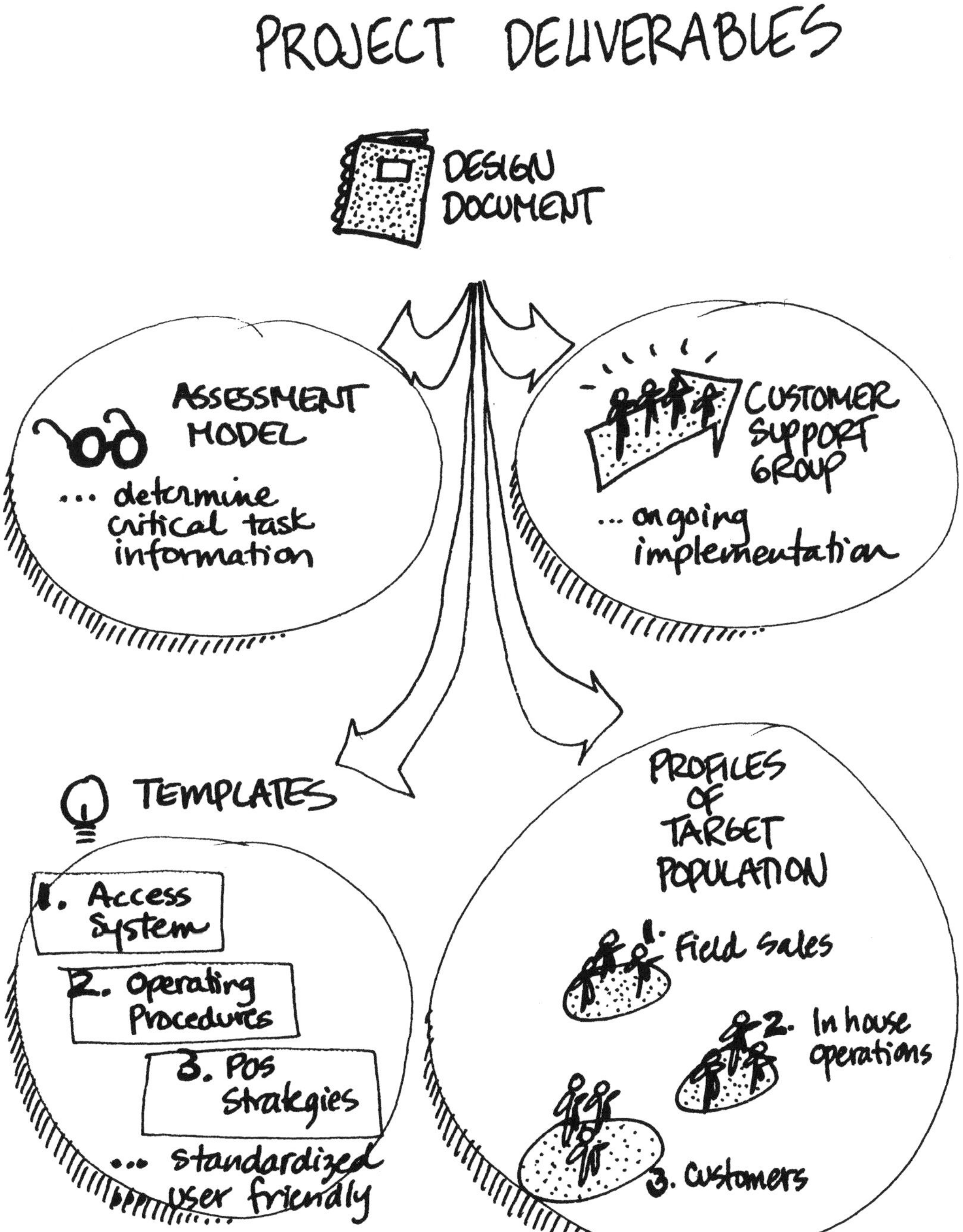
PROJECT DELIVERABLES
DESIGN DOCUMENT
ASSESSMENT MODEL
... determine critical task information
CUSTOMER SUPPORT GROUP
... ongoing implementation
TEMPLATES
1. Access System
2. Operating Procedures
3. Pos Strategies
... standardized user friendly
PROFILES OF TARGET POPULATION
1. Field sales
2. In house operations
3. Customers

Notetaking from class presentation. Pen highlighted with colored pencils. Original size: 8 1/2 x 11 bound journal.

CONSULTING SKILLS
* looking at roles
* looking at contracting
"Getting ahead and esteem are related"
Maslow's hierarchy
I want interesting work
Values
STAFF ROLE
Safety Issues
Influence without direct CONTROL
SIGNS of CONTROL Line Manager
• The illusion of direct control
* Give up the control, gain a certain amount of freedom
• Line manager heaven is to do the same things over and over with no people....!
* No control: certain impotence
* For us to function people (managers) have to put their worst foot foward
Acting as a partner
HOW TO BE A PARTNER WITH PEOPLE WHO OWN YOU...
* The control we have is to withhold service
when we are not
INTERNAL COMMITMENT
CREDIBILITY
...the cheapest thing they have to spend on us is money....
CHOICE & SAYING NO
Need to have the right to say no
TRUST
can they lean on you?
RESPONSIBILITY
...How is it shared...
50 50
90 10
10 90
• Consulting firms move this direction
Bent over Position

BIBLIOGRAPHY

BOOKS on DRAWING

• *Drawing with Children* by Mona Brookes. Published by J. P. Tarcher, Inc., Los Angeles, CA, 1986.

Brookes has developed practices for drawing that focus on the ability to perceive shapes. Her book is filled with good information and useful exercises for children and adults.

• *Drawing on the Right Side of the Brain* by Betty Edwards. Published by J. P. Tarcher, Inc., Los Angeles, CA, 1979.

This is the book that really made believers of us that "drawing is seeing". Lots of exercises and good information.

• *Ed Emberley's Drawing Book: Make a World* by Ed Emberley. Published by Little, Brown and Company, Boston, MA, 1972.

A great book that Ed Emberley has created for children and we're encouraging adults to ask their children to share with them. Emberley shows us how to draw hundreds of objects by building on shapes and lines, i.e., essence. This book is useful for anyone who wants to create drawings on the Macintosh Mac Draw program.

• *Mark Kistler's Draw Squad* by Mark Kistler. Published by Simon & Schuster, New York, NY, 1988.

Another book for children and adults - anyone who wants to have a lot of fun learning to draw.

BOOKS on CARTOONING

• *Cartooning the Head and Figure.* by Jack Hamm. Published by Grosset & Dunlap, New York, NY, 1967.

Lots of stuff about cartooning. What we like best about this book is lots of faces and lots of figures from a variety of positions.

• *How to be a Cartoonist* by Peter Maddocks. Published by Simon & Schuster, New York, NY, 1982.

A clear, simple presentation of basics...faces, hands and actions.

FLIP CHART GRAPHICS

• *Fundamentals of Graphic Language: Practice Book* (2nd ed.) by David Sibbet. Published by Grove Consultants International, San Francisco, CA, 1993.

A great practice book for the wonderful system and processes David Sibbet has developed for "Group Graphics!"

• *Flip Charts: How to Draw Them and How to Use Them* by Richard C. Brandt. Published by Pfeiffer & Company, San Diego, CA, 1986.

Richard Brandt has done a great job of presenting everything you wanted to know about flip charts!

• *Field Guide to Flip Charts* by Jennifer Hammond Landau and Jean Westcott, 1987. Available from Jean Westcott and Jennifer Hammond Landau, 1697 Oak Street, San Francisco, CA. 94117, (415) 255 - 2893 or (510) 536 - 1657).

This pocket-sized booklet summarizes all of the skills you need to create flip charts.

BOOKS on COMPUTERS (and selection of Typefaces)

• *Looking Good in Print -A Guide to Basic Design for Desktop Publishing* by Roger C. Parker. Published by Ventana Press, Chapel Hill, NC, 1988.

Parker takes his own advice in designing pages that are easy to read. Great tips on page design and the value of restraint.

• *Designing with Type* by James Craig. Published by Watson-Guptill, New York, NY, 1980.

The author describes the characteristices of many typefaces and suggests when each is best used.

• *The Typefaces of Desktop Publishing* by Craig Danuloff and Deke McClelland. Published by Publishing Resources, Boulder, CO, 1987.

A very useful catalog that includes most of the typefaces available on the Macintosh. They include a full alphabet for each type face and useful hints on choices/selection.

MISCELLANEOUS

• *The First Thousand Words* by Heather Amery and Stephen Cartwright. Published by Mayflower Books, New York, NY, 1979.

The idea of this book is to have some fun as kids learn to read -- and it is fun. The bonus for adults is there are lots of simple drawings of objects and people. NOTE: other kid's dictionaries can be great resources...check out the pictures, and grab the ones that use simple line drawings!

• *Handbook of Pictorial Symbols* by Rudolf Modley. Published by Dover Publications, Inc., New York, NY. 1976.

Exactly what the title suggests.... this is a great collection of graphic symbols, many of them used internationally.

• *The Book of Graphic Problem Solving - How to Get Visual Ideas When You Need Them* by John Newcomb. Published by R.R. Bowker Company, New York, NY, 1984.

When you really begin to have some serious fun in adding graphics to your presentations, this is a great resource. Newcomb shows you the thinking and drawing steps he used to create many of his best graphic images.

• *Ready to Use Humorous Illustrations* by Edward Sibbett. Published by Dover Publications, Inc., New York, NY, 1984.

This is one of several Dover clip art publications. They are the least expensive clip art we know of... and include cartoon style drawings (vs. more complex illustrations).

This list would not be complete if we did not include the most available, least expensive source of graphic symbols that we know about, i.e., The Yellow Pages of your local telephone directory.

9 780787 903527

953461

Printed in Great Britain by
Amazon.co.uk, Ltd.,
Marston Gate.